And then Ben received the biggest shock of all. Jane shifted position, as if to ease her cramped limbs. At once there was movement across the room: the guard was alert. But luckily, he could not hear what followed.

"In my left shoe – behind my heel," she murmured. "Take it! It will help answer those who doubt you – for someone must reveal what Sir Miles is doing. Can't you see that?" She was desperate now. "I've no one else to turn to, Ben Button, so I must trust you!"

For Freya, when she's old enough

First published in the UK in 2009 by Usborne Publishing Ltd., Usborne House, 83-85 Saffron Hill, London EC1N 8RT, England. www.usborne.com

Copyright © John Pilkington, 2009

The right of John Pilkington to be identified as the author of this work has been asserted by him in accordance with the Copyright, Designs and Patents Act, 1988.

Cover artwork by Michael Thompson. Map by Ian McNee.

The name Usborne and the devices ♀ 🜨 are Trade Marks of Usborne Publishing Ltd.

A CIP catalogue record for this book is available from the British Library.

J MAMJJASOND/09 88839 ISBN 9780746097984 Printed in Great Britain.

ELIZABETHAN MYSTERIES

Revenge!

JOHN
PILKINGTON

USBORNE

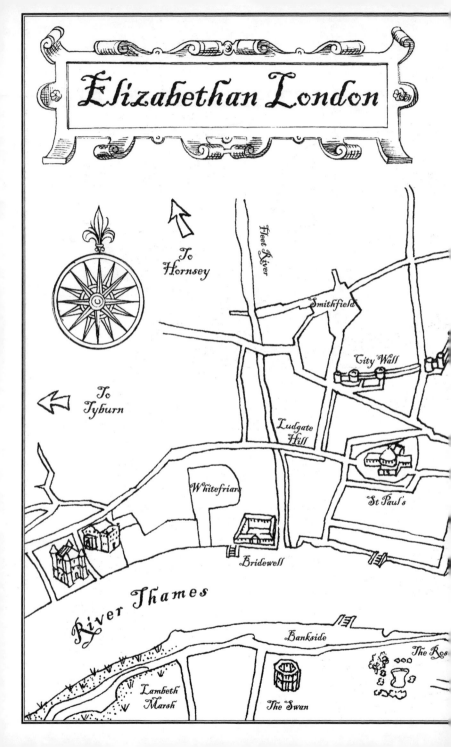

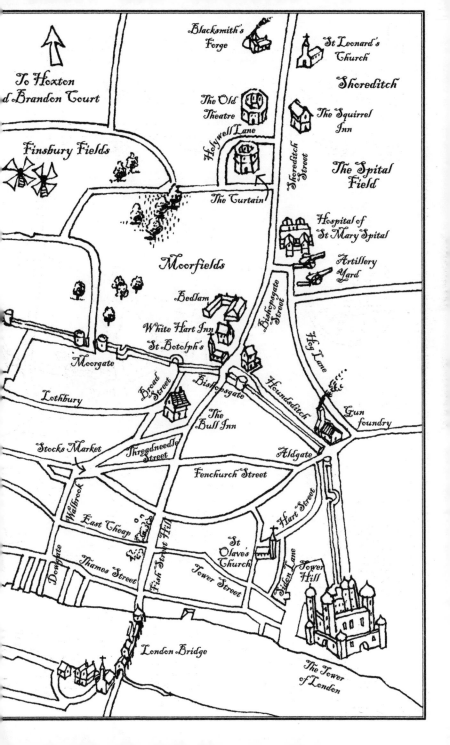

Chapter One

There was no escaping it: Ben Button would have to have his tooth pulled out.

It may have been a bright spring morning, but Ben hardly noticed. And he may have been Master Ben Button, featured actor with the famous Lord Bonner's company of players – but just now he felt like any boy with a toothache. In the last two days the ache had worsened, until even the thought of brawny Ned Campion getting his pincers on it seemed better than the pain. So at his master John Symes's bidding, Ben set out alone from their house on the corner of Hog Lane and Bishopsgate Street and started northwards towards Shoreditch – and towards Ned.

Ned Campion was the blacksmith, whose forge stood by the roadside opposite St Leonard's church. He was also the village tooth-drawer, a task he rather enjoyed. Ben had seen grown men come out of Ned's, hands over their mouths, grunting with pain. Sometimes the blacksmith's noisy laugh followed them outside.

"Call yourself a man?" Ned would shout. "Children make far less fuss! Stop whining and get back to work!"

Despite his ache, Ben smiled at the memory. The April sunshine was warm, and he loosened his cherry-red doublet. He passed the turning to Finsbury Fields on his left. People walked by: housewives with baskets heading for the city markets, a man leading a horse out to pasture, two boys with longbows going into the Fields to practise their archery. One of them knew Ben, and gave him greeting. There was also a pedlar with a huge pack on his back, tramping away from London to sell his wares in the country.

Even from half a mile away, the hum of the great capital reached Ben's ears. The population, it was said, had now swelled to two hundred thousand people, making it one of the biggest cities in Europe. In fact London had grown so much that it was spreading far beyond the old walls. Shoreditch, once a tiny village, and even Hoxton further off, were becoming busy suburbs. Noblemen had built summer houses here, north of the city, where the air was sweet and filled with birdsong. And though Ben missed his own village of Hornsey sometimes, and his mother, brother and sister too, he took comfort from the Fields, with the sails of windmills turning in the distance. The mills always reminded him of home. John Symes, the company's leading player and Ben's master, had promised that he could visit his family in the summer. It was a long time since he had seen them, and he looked forward eagerly to the trip.

There was a shout. Ben had reached Holywell Lane, which led to his current place of work: the Curtain Theatre. He looked to his left and saw someone waving at him – and at once he forgot about his appointment with Ned Campion and his pincers, and hurried along the lane.

"You're up early, young master," the man said as Ben drew close. "I thought you player folk stayed in bed all morning!"

The speaker was a scrawny fellow in baggy taffeta

breeches and a patched shirt with sleeves rolled to the elbows. He wore an old hat and carried a pole over his shoulder, from which hung the limp carcasses of several black rats. Tom Slyte the rat-catcher, with his bushy beard and lopsided grin, was a well-known figure about the suburbs. Ben had got to know him soon after coming here, when he first became a player with Lord Bonner's Men. Ben had been in the Fields walking Brutus, the Symes family's old hound, when a little terrier had run up, barking fiercely. Brutus had growled back, and a fight might have broken out if Tom had not appeared and called his dog to heel. Since then the two of them often laughed about how funny Tom's dog Peascod had looked, yapping at Brutus, who was twice his size and could have picked him up easily in his jaws.

"Good day, Master Tom," Ben said. "Where's Peascod?"

Tom shrugged. "I don't know... He wanders off where he will these days." The rat-catcher pointed. "I'm for Shoreditch – will you walk with me?"

Ben was glad of some company to take his mind off the tooth. As they fell into step, Tom's talk soon turned to the topic of rats, on which he was, of course, an expert.

"I've got as much work as I can deal with this

spring," he said. "No matter how many of the varlets I despatch, there seem to be more of 'em about. Now folk in Shoreditch say there's loaves gone from a bakehouse..." He shook his head. "If you ask me, that's naught to do with rats. Thieves that walk on two legs, more like!"

There was an excited bark from behind. Ben turned as Peascod came bounding towards him, and stopped to greet the ragged little terrier, who began leaping up, trying to lick his face.

"Save us, Master Tom," Ben said, wrinkling his nose. "When did you last give your friend a bath?"

"He don't like baths, any more than I do," Tom muttered. "Waste of time. Though I did have one last Christmas, to please my landlord. Said my chamber was the worst in the house... I mean, what does he expect? I'm a rat-catcher, not the Lord Chamberlain!"

It was well known that Tom was not the cleanest of men. But seeing the indignant look on his face, Ben felt a laugh coming on. Quickly he turned it into a cough.

They had turned into Shoreditch Street, where there were a few folk walking. No doubt thinking it was time to drum up business, Tom drew a deep breath and called out his famous chant:

"Rats or mice! Have ye any rats or mice?
Have ye moles, polecats or weasels?
I'll kill the vermin that run down the holes,
And cure a sow sick of the measles!"

"Can you really cure a sow of the measles?" Ben asked him, in an innocent voice.

"It rhymes with *weasels*, Master Ben," Tom replied, grinning at him through his scraggy beard. "I couldn't think what else to put in."

Ben laughed aloud this time, then winced as his toothache came back. He put his hand to his jaw. Tom had stopped walking, and was looking over his shoulder towards two of the most famous buildings north of the city: the Old Theatre and the Curtain, which stood on either side of the lane, barely a hundred yards apart.

"Talking of the Lord Chamberlain," Tom said, "I hear his players are packing folk in over there, like stockfish in a barrel. Is that so?"

Ben's company were performing at the Curtain at present, while the most famous players of all, the Lord Chamberlain's Men, were using the bigger building, which nowadays people called the Old Theatre.

"The Chamberlain's Men have a new play called *Romeo and Juliet*, written by Master Shakespeare,"

Ben said. "I hear it's a good piece."

He fell silent. The truth was, there was strong competition between the two Shoreditch theatres. Though there were enough eager Londoners to fill both the Old Theatre and the Curtain on a fine afternoon, in bad weather audiences dwindled, and Lord Bonner's Men were hard pressed to cover their costs. Things were always difficult around this time, for during the forty days of Lent, up until Easter, the theatres had to close down by law. But now they had reopened, and the company were relieved to see crowds streaming out of the city again.

The silence was broken by Peascod barking and racing off. Tom sighed – then at last noticed Ben's discomfort.

"Does something ail you?" he enquired. "If it does, I carry a few cures here…" He patted his belt, from which hung several small bags and pouches. "Cloves to chew, to take away pain. Or I've a blend of herbs, lavender and rue and such – good for a headache."

They were walking between houses roofed with thatch. Ahead, the tower of St Leonard's church loomed above the rooftops. Its famous bells had become fixed in the old rhyme that children sang:

"Old Father Baldpate," say the slow bells of Aldgate;
"You owe me ten shillings," say the bells of St Helen's.

"When will you pay me?" say the bells of Old Bailey;

"When I grow rich," say the bells of Shoreditch.

But now, from near the church, came not the sound of bells, but the loud clang of a hammer beating upon an iron anvil. Ben gave a sigh: Ned Campion awaited him. He turned to say farewell to Tom, and found the rat-catcher's gaze upon him.

"I should 'a' guessed." Tom jerked his head in the direction of the blacksmith's. "One of your pegs got to come out, has it?" He grinned. "I'll wager just now you'd rather stick your hand in a fire than step inside old Ned's place – do I hit the mark?"

Ben nodded, and trudged off towards his doom.

A short while later he was sat on a stool at the rear of the forge. He had taken off his doublet and opened his shirt, but still the heat of the blazing charcoal furnace was so fierce it almost made him dizzy. Close by, Ned's huge leather bellows hissed, worked by his prentice, a portly boy named Martin. Ned himself, grey-haired and grey-bearded, was bare to the waist and shiny with sweat. He eyed Ben as he wiped his hands on his breeches.

"I'll make no charge for ye, master player," he said

cheerfully. "Best laugh I've had in months, seeing your company at the Curtain yesterday. That ghost near scared me to death! I told Master Symes, if any of you folk want a tooth drawn, you come to me – even the ghost!"

The play Lord Bonner's Men were performing just now was called *The Old Wives' Tale*, and Ben was taking the part of Delia, who was held captive by a sinister magician until she was rescued by a brave knight. Playing the female roles, of course, was Ben's job, as it was for all boy actors, since women were not permitted on the stage. There was also a ghost in the play – a role which Solomon Tree, the company's comedian, was getting bored with playing. Lately he had taken to coming onstage by different entrances, drawing screams from the audience. He had even tried to scare the other players by hiding in a corner of the tiring room and leaping out with arms raised. But since nobody took any notice, he soon abandoned the idea.

Ned had reached up the wall, and was taking down something that every village child, and many a grown man and woman too, dreaded: a pair of heavy pincers, wrought by his own hands. "Well, young master..." Ned snapped the pincers shut, like a giant crab's claw. "Are you ready?"

With a gulp, Ben opened his mouth and closed his eyes, steeling himself for the pain.

"Not yet!"

He opened his eyes again, to find Ned bending over him.

"Hadn't you better tell me which one hurts?" the smith asked, and broke into his famous laugh. Like a donkey braying for its dinner, someone had once said.

Ben touched a top tooth, to the left of his front ones, and Ned peered into his mouth. "Ah – one of your dog teeth! I pull plenty of those." Without warning he stuck his fingers in and grabbed the tooth, making Ben flinch.

"Aye...that's the culprit!" Ned lifted his pincers again. "Now you can shut your eyes, if you like!"

No sooner had Ben done so than Ned's great calloused hand was clamped firmly about his jaws, forcing them wide apart. He felt the coldness of the pincers as they pressed against his gums...there was a scrape of iron as they closed on his tooth – then with enormous force it was wrenched out. Ben had one moment of harsh pain before opening his eyes, to see Ned flourishing the pincers which held his tooth, blood-red at its root.

"Well done!" Ned nodded his approval. "You're

a plucky fellow, Master Ben, and that's a fact."

Though he tasted blood, Ben's relief was great. He knew the pain would lessen soon. He looked round to see tubby Martin holding out a bit of linen.

"Best staunch it with this," he said in his high voice. Martin was known about Shoreditch as Squeaky.

Taking the cloth, Ben held it to his mouth and stood up. "I thank you, Master Ned," he said. "It was very quick."

The blacksmith wiped Ben's tooth on his breeches and handed it to him. "Keep that," he said. "It might bring you luck." Then he glanced at Squeaky Martin, who was still standing by. "What are you about?" he cried. "That fire's sinking – get back on the bellows!" As Martin scurried off to his work, Ned turned to Ben, shaking his head.

"He'd do naught all day if I didn't watch him," he said, "apart from eating!" Then a thought struck him. "Here, I've just remembered. Is it true you're singing at the church in a few weeks? For the Whitsun Ale?"

"The whole company's performing," Ben answered. "We'll be playing and singing." All of Shoreditch was looking forward to Whitsuntide, when specially brewed ale would be sold in the churchyard to raise money for St Leonard's. It was a good excuse for a village fair.

"Well, now..." Ned broke into a smile. "Then I do believe you'll have some competition!"

Seeing the puzzled look on Ben's face, the brawny smith laughed and clapped him on the back. "I don't mean from human players – these are but puppets!"

He turned away to resume his work. And with Master Campion's laughter still ringing in his ears, Ben took his farewell.

He walked homeward, thinking over what Ned had told him. It was the first he had heard about a puppet show coming to Shoreditch. He wondered if John Symes knew. For if the puppet man was the one he thought it might be...well, the news was not entirely welcome. In fact, it could even spell trouble.

Soon he was hurrying back towards Hog Lane, the pain where his tooth had once been now forgotten.

Chapter Two

"Harry Higgs?" John Symes was frowning. "I didn't think he'd show his face here again so soon."

He and Ben were sitting in the kitchen, taking a drink before setting off for the theatre. Ben had related Ned Campion's news, and it caused John some dismay. It was the first time the name of Harry Higgs had been spoken in the Symes's house for some time.

"It may not be him," Ben said, and drained his mug. He had been very thirsty since his visit to

Ned's. "There are other puppet masters, aren't there?"

"Indeed – but something in my bones tells me it's Higgs." John sighed. "Now I'm sounding like Solomon, with his predictions of doom."

Ben remembered Master Higgs well – as did all of Lord Bonner's Men. He was a crafty rogue, with more tricks up his sleeve than a conjuror. Last spring he had appeared with his brightly coloured puppet theatre and set it up in Finsbury Fields, where people heading for the theatres would have to pass by. There he waylaid the crowds, inviting poorer folk to see his show for whatever they could afford instead of paying a penny to enter the theatre yard. So good a showman was Higgs that many, young and old alike, stopped to watch his puppet play – it was *Gawain and the Green Knight*, Ben remembered – instead of going to the Curtain to watch Lord Bonner's Men.

But that was just the start of it. When the company's bookkeeper Will Sanders told the puppet man he wasn't welcome, the two of them had come to blows, which had left Will with a sore head – something he had not forgotten.

"Well, then…" John emptied his own mug and set it down. "Let's say it's Higgs. If so, he's welcome at the Whitsun Ale – but if he sets up outside the theatre and steals our crowd, that's another matter. We'll find a way to make him take his puppets somewhere else – even if I have to pay him off!" He shook his head. "This is all we need, with the theatre's rent due, and you and Matt both needing new attire. Can't you boys stop growing?"

Ben grinned. It was true that he had grown an inch or so since the winter, while his fellow boy player Matt Fields was "shooting up like a beanstalk", as Will Sanders put it. The tailor's bill for new costumes to fit them both was a source of constant grumbling from Will.

The front door was heard opening, followed by rapid footsteps in the passage. John's daughter Meg came running in.

"Father, is it true what they say – that the puppet man's coming to the Whitsun Ale?" Ten-year-old Meg's face was bright with excitement. Her older sister Kate, who was closer to Ben's age, followed her in.

"It seems so, rosy one." John smiled as he pinched Meg's cheek. Then his smile faded. "But if that old rogue sets up by the theatre again, I'll be having words with him – and I wouldn't want to see you two girls among his audience. You can wait until Whitsun, can't you? There'll likely be morris dancers and jugglers too – and Lord Bonner's players, of course. Is that not something to look forward to?"

Meg nodded, still beaming with delight.

"That's cheered her up," Kate said with a smile. "She was near to tears an hour ago, because she couldn't go with Mother to East Cheap."

"I was not!" Meg's smile vanished. "Anyway, she said I can go next week, and choose a new kirtle." Then, remembering Ben's trip to the blacksmith, she looked curiously at him. "Is your tooth out?"

Ben opened his mouth to show the gap. Then he took the tooth from his pocket and held it up. Both girls gazed at it with interest.

"Did it hurt much?" Kate asked.

"Only for a moment," Ben said, with a shrug.

"Well, at least it's over and done with." John stood up. "Now it's time we were off to the Curtain. The crowds will be gathering – or at least, I hope they will."

"Why do they call it that?" Meg asked, ever the curious one. "I've always wondered. There are no curtains. Except those over the doors to the tiring room."

"It's named after the land it was built on," Kate said. "The curtain wall of the old priory once stood there."

"I knew that!" Meg retorted, somewhat untruthfully.

"Here – no arguing, if you please." John wore a stern expression, but Ben knew how much he delighted in his lively daughters. "Your mother will be back at any moment," he added. "Will you go to the door and see?"

The girls made obedient curtsies to their father. But as they turned to go out, Ben heard Meg whisper: "Anyway, long before there was a priory, Bishopsgate Street was a Roman road – did you know *that*?"

He glanced at his master, and saw him hiding a smile.

That day was a Wednesday. In the afternoon Lord Bonner's Men made the most of the fine weather, playing to a packed theatre. *The Old Wives' Tale,* written by a witty playmaker called George Peele, was a favourite with the crowds. At the end of the performance, the audience roared their approval – but they did not quite drown out the noise from the Old Theatre a hundred yards away, where *Romeo and Juliet* was still in full flow. And as the company took their bows and left the stage for the tiring room, Solomon Tree insisted on reminding everyone what a success the Chamberlain's Men's new play was.

"Romance – that's what folk want nowadays," he said. "A tale of doomed lovers who die at the end, and make everyone weep enough to fill the town ditch – I mean, where's the comedy?" He gazed mournfully around the crowded room. "Isn't there enough gloom in the world as it is?"

"There's certainly no shortage with you about," Gabriel Tucker said wryly. The twitchy little player who took the villain roles was in good spirits, having given a fine, moustache-curling performance as Sacrapant the magician.

"There's truth in Sol's words, though."

The others looked at Hugh Cotton, their leading player, known these days as Handsome Hugh, who was of course taking the part of the brave knight.

"A few years back," Hugh went on, "all the crowd wanted was history plays, with banners and battles. Now we've had poor harvests and plague – not to mention war with Spain. Do you wonder if tastes are changing? Folk want romance to escape their troubles – and I for one don't blame them."

It was true, though the ever-present threat from the Spanish foe was something no one wished to dwell on.

"We give them enough to forget their troubles,"

John said. He was taking off his costume, helped by Will Sanders, who was muttering into his beard. Finally John looked round with a frown.

"What are you fretting about, master grumbler?"

Will grunted. "It makes me uneasy when I hear talk like that," he said. "Next you'll all be clamouring for another new play by Peele, or Daniel Rix, or... someone, and that'll be pounds gone from our coffer! Can't we make do with the ones we've got?"

Everyone knew that plays were expensive. But they took many months and a great deal of skill to write, and only clever poets could do it – like Master Shakespeare, the cleverest of all.

"I believe we *can* make do," Gabriel said, sticking his puny chest out. "Did you not hear the applause today? We may have rivals, but we can still fill the Curtain – yard *and* galleries too!" He looked round defiantly. "And why should we care if Harry Higgs is coming back to Shoreditch, as folk say? Are we afraid of puppets now?"

There was some laughter. Even Solomon seemed cheered. And soon after, the players began taking their leave. Ben finished changing, and handed his splendid Delia costume – an elaborate pink gown – to Will. When Matt Fields came up to say he was going to watch an archery practice, Ben agreed to tag along.

Promising John that he would be home in an hour, he followed Matt outside into the lane. Finsbury Fields stretched westward, with the sun low in the sky.

Ben and Matt had become close friends since the danger they had shared last winter on Bankside, when the ruthless Earl of Horsham had had them both kidnapped to try and prevent Lord Bonner's Men from performing for the Queen. The two of them still argued, but it was no more than banter. In fact, it was one way of amusing themselves during those tedious times when there were no performances, and they had to run errands or do chores for the company. Mercifully the idle days of Lent were just a memory now, and a busy time lay before them.

"Well – look who's there." Matt nodded towards a group of people standing by the pathway. From their appearance, they were beggars – the ragged folk who stood in London's streets and markets calling for charity, and who sometimes gathered near the theatres. But the figure who had caught Matt's eye, and now Ben's, was a heavyset fellow in a padded jerkin and an old feathered hat: James Plugg, the constable of Shoreditch. A man whom few liked, and who was mocked behind his back for his slowness, as well as for his sheer dullness.

"Master Plugg – a fine evening, is it not?" With a

mischievous glance at Ben, Matt approached the constable. Ben followed, trying not to laugh. Matt never missed a chance to go Plugg-baiting, as he called it. At the sound of his voice, Shoreditch's champion of the law turned to them both with a sour expression.

"You two again!" Plugg waved a finger at them. "On your way – I'm busy."

"Busy?" Matt was wearing his innocent face. "What's the trouble? Perhaps we can be of assistance."

The constable's thick eyebrows moved together like furry caterpillars. "The only time I'll need assistance from you – or any of you popinjays – is when I arrest you for...for something or other," Plugg growled. "Now get along!" And with that, he turned away.

Now that Ben had chance to look closely at the beggars, he was moved to pity, as he always was at the sight of such people. One fellow in heavily patched clothes, who had lost an arm, looked like an ex-soldier. His empty sleeve was folded and pinned up. Another man was blind, his eyes as cloudy as milk. He carried a wooden bowl, in which lay but a few farthings. There was a woman too, as thin as a rake and swaddled in rags. Then Ben's glance fell upon the last member of the group – and there it stayed. For this one was of a different stamp.

He was a boy, perhaps a year younger than Ben, in a dirty jerkin and breeches too big for him. His shoes were worn out, and full of holes. On his head was a shapeless woollen cap, pulled low over the ears. He wore no hose, and his bare legs were dirty, with great sores upon them. Feeling Ben's eyes upon him, the lad met his gaze, then looked away – but not before Ben had caught an odd expression on his face.

It was this boy, Ben and Matt realized, who had caught Constable Plugg's attention. And since the constable had been distracted by their arrival, the other beggars had begun to make themselves scarce. The ex-soldier spoke to the blind man, who took hold of his sleeve and followed him. The woman was already shuffling away. But Plugg did not seem interested, which must have been a relief. Vagrants caught begging without a licence, or merely wandering outside their own parishes, could be whipped, even burned through the ear or branded. Some constables simply sent them on their way, but others – like Master Plugg – were as likely to put the unfortunate folk in the stocks, or deal them a harsh flogging. Towering over the boy with the sores, he leaned down and pushed his face close.

"I haven't seen you before, have I, young master?" he said. "What are you doing in my parish?"

The lad swallowed. His gaze strayed briefly towards Ben and Matt, then dropped.

"I asked you a question, child!" Plugg barked. "And how did ye get those sores?"

Suddenly, the ragged boy seemed to find his voice. "Scalded, sir!" he cried. "When my house burned down, back in the Midlands. Burned right to the ground! Will you not pity poor Tobias? My mother and father, brothers and sisters – all were lost, sir! Only I survived, with but the clothes on my back, and no one to take me in. Show mercy, master, for 'tis the truth – every word!"

"Truth?" Plugg sneered. "Don't lie to me, ye little stoat – I know all the tricks you folk get up to!" He pointed to the boy's leg, and a grim smile appeared on his face. "Shall I tell ye how you got those wounds? You put spearwort leaves on your skin, to make it blister! Then you rubbed charcoal in, to make it look worse!" The constable jerked his thumb at Ben and Matt, who stood by in silence. "Why – you ought to take up with these two rogues, for you're as good a play-actor as they are!"

He gave a mirthless laugh. But his eyes remained fixed upon Tobias, alert for any movement. The boy sensed that escape was all but impossible, and a frightened look came over him. Which was all the two young players needed to spur them into action.

"Oh, my – did you say spearwort?" Matt Fields's hand flew to his mouth, as he stared in horror at the beggar's sores. "That's terrible – it makes me go weak at the knees! Help!"

Constable Plugg rotated his solid frame towards Matt. "I told ye last time," he cried, "if you ever mocked me again, I'd arrest you and give you half a dozen strokes of the lash…"

But he broke off, as Matt's eyes rolled up under his eyelids, and a gurgling sound came from his mouth. The boy staggered, then collapsed on the ground, twitching. Ben had to admit to himself that it was a good performance.

"Get up, ye young fool!" Plugg shouted. He peered down at Matt, who was groaning – and taking his cue, Ben seized the moment. Sidestepping the constable, he grabbed the startled Tobias by the arm and bent close. "Run!" he whispered. "And don't look back!"

For a second the boy hesitated. Then, with a glance at Plugg, he took to his heels and sprinted across Finsbury Fields like a hare. And if there had been any doubt as to whether his leg wounds were real or not, it soon vanished. The beggar boy was a fake – as his tale of home and family being lost in a fire was likely a fake, too.

Ben watched him run until he was a distant blur. He knew about false beggars and their tricks: like those who feigned madness, or those who pretended to be lame... Yet this wiry boy, with his baggy clothes and his plaintive voice, intrigued him. Why that should be, he did not know.

But he felt sure of one thing: whatever Tobias had done, he did not deserve a flogging at the hands of Constable Plugg.

Chapter Three

The next morning Ben was up early, taking Brutus for his usual walk in Finsbury Fields. The old hound ambled through the grass, sniffing at everything; he liked nothing more than to be out with Ben, his firm friend. The day was cloudy, and Ben eyed the skies warily: a storm could mean a cancelled performance at the Curtain. He knew what he would have to do if that happened: dancing practice. Not that he disliked the jigs and hornpipes Lord Bonner's Men danced, usually after the play was over. It was simply that for Ben, acting was more important than almost anything – better than dancing at least, or studying the lute. John was a fine lutenist, who was now passing on his skills to Ben. There were many things a boy player had to learn – even how to fake having a fit, as Matt had done, Ben thought with a smile. He was glad they had helped the beggar boy escape Plugg's clutches yesterday. Even if the constable was furious, and had vowed to pay them back the first chance he got.

He was jolted out of his thoughts by Brutus straining at the leash. Ben untied it from his collar, and let him trot away. Following the old dog, he crossed the path that led northwards from Moorgate, all the way out to Hoxton. Before him stood the windmills, their huge sails drifting slowly around in the light breeze. Ben had stopped to gaze at them when a bark from behind made him turn: it was Peascod. Beside him, Tom Slyte stood with his pole on his shoulder, empty of rats this time. Ben waved, and walked towards them.

"I heard someone's been sleeping in one of the mills," Tom said, and gave a shrug. "Vagrants, passing through, would be my guess. There are so many about nowadays – discharged soldiers and sailors, with nowhere to go." He sighed. "Not that I condemn them, Master Ben. Small thanks they got for seeing off the Spaniards, back when we all thought we'd be invaded. You'd think the country would show more gratitude, now wouldn't ye?"

Ben had been only a small child when the great Spanish Armada sailed up the English Channel. But he well remembered the fear that swept through the land, as he remembered the men of his own village, his father among them, mustering on the green with their pikes. Every town and village had raised militia to defend the country. Mercifully, strong winds, together with the cunning and bravery of the English seamen, had seen off the huge galleons and sent them floundering up the North Sea, running out of food and water as well as gunpowder. But the Spanish threat could never be forgotten: no one knew when England's most dangerous foe might strike again.

There was another bark, and Ben looked round. "Brutus," he said. "I'd almost forgotten him."

He got the leash ready, but as the old hound ran up, he hesitated. Brutus was panting excitedly. He barked, darted off, then turned and barked again.

"What's bothering him?" Tom asked.

"I don't know," Ben replied. "But something is."

Brutus bounded away again. It was clear that he had seen something, so with a wave at the rat-catcher, Ben hurried off in pursuit.

They ran across the Fields, joining the lane that led all the way to Smithfield. There were hedges on either side here, with fair gardens behind them. Suddenly Brutus stopped and lowered his head, peering between the bars of a gate. Somewhat out of breath, Ben came up beside him and looked through the gateway.

The garden within was overgrown, and the large house beyond was silent, the windows shuttered. Whoever the owners were, they must be absent. Then Ben's gaze fell upon a dog kennel with a pitched roof, standing to one side of the gate.

"So that's what interested you," he said, looking down at Brutus. "Well, if a friend of yours lives there, he's likely gone away with his master."

But the old dog growled, and his ears pricked up.

"Look – it's empty," Ben told him. Picking up a stone, he lobbed it onto the roof of the doghouse. Whereupon there came a cry from inside, which startled Ben as much as it did Brutus.

"Leave me alone!" someone shouted. "And call your hound off!"

Brutus barked loudly, and would have tried to scramble under the gate if Ben had not grabbed his collar. Quickly he knotted the leash to it.

"It's all right," he called, feeling rather foolish to be talking to someone he could not see. "I've tied him up – he wouldn't harm you, in any case."

There was a shuffling from inside the kennel. Two feet clad in old, worn-out shoes appeared, then a pair of bare legs covered with sores...and Ben gave a start. Even before the shabby figure of Tobias the beggar had eased himself out, Ben knew it was him. In a moment the ragged boy had got to his feet, and the two of them were looking at each other over the gate. Brutus barked again.

"I've done nothing!" Tobias cried. "Don't set him on me!"

"Of course I won't," Ben said, and kneeled down beside the old hound. After he had spoken softly to him, Brutus calmed down, and stood looking at the beggar boy with a puzzled expression.

Then all at once Tobias recognized Ben. "I saw you yesterday, by the theatre," he said.

"What were you doing in there?" Ben asked him, nodding towards the dog kennel.

The other gave a shrug. "I didn't take anything," he muttered.

"No one said you did," Ben replied. Looking closely at the beggar, he thought once again that there was something odd about him.

"Move aside, will you?" Tobias said. "Then I'll be on my way."

Holding Brutus's leash, Ben stepped back from the gate while Tobias clambered over it. Then, with his arms wrapped about his body as if he were cold, he glanced up and down the lane.

"I've no money with me," Ben said, meaning to help the boy. "Yet if you care to come to my master's house, he may spare you a penny."

But Tobias shook his head. "I've got business," he said shortly. With that he turned – whereupon there came a sound that made Ben's ears prick up as well as Brutus's: a clank of metal. And it seemed to come from the direction of Tobias's baggy breeches.

In an instant, Ben understood. "You've burgled that house!" he cried. "That's why you hid in the kennel – Brutus saw you come out!"

But even before he had finished speaking, Tobias had turned to flee. And remembering the speed he had shown the day before, Ben knew it would be hard to catch him.

"Whatever you've taken, drop it," he said. "Or I'll let the dog loose!"

Tobias took no notice. Instead he clutched his breeches, which bulged with something concealed, and ran off awkwardly, back along the lane towards the Fields.

"Stop!" Ben shouted, and bent to untie Brutus,

who was tugging at the leash. Then looking up, he saw the beggar stumble to a halt. Two large silver goblets fell from his clothing, and clattered to the ground. Hurriedly the boy stooped to pick them up – which gave Ben his chance. Leaving Brutus, he covered the short distance between himself and Tobias, and made a grab for him – which failed, for the other merely dodged aside, and planted a vicious kick on Ben's shin.

"Ow!" It was Ben's turn to stumble, as pain shot through his leg. He grabbed hold of it, wincing, while the beggar retrieved the stolen goblets. Without looking back at Ben, he veered away and ran.

But things did not go well for him now, for there were people in the Fields: two women carrying a basket of laundry, and a man with a hunting dog on a rope. Hearing the commotion, they stopped to look. Meanwhile Brutus bounded past Ben, leash trailing, ready to leap at Tobias's back.

Hearing Brutus behind him, the beggar skidded to a halt and turned round. But the old hound was not as agile as he had once been, and when he jumped, Tobias was able to duck. At once he started off again – in the direction Ben least expected: along the lane towards him.

"Out of my way!" the beggar yelled, and raised a

fist. But this time Ben was quicker. He stepped back as if to let the other pass – then stuck a foot out and tripped him. With a yelp, Tobias fell face-first into the grass. Yet somehow he managed to hold onto the goblets and wriggle away from Ben. He was soon scrambling to his feet again and, with Ben close behind, he raced away down the lane.

But he had only a slight start, and Ben was not about to give up now. With eyes fixed upon Tobias, he speeded up until he was sprinting faster than he had run in years. Then at last, judging the distance, he launched himself through the air, arms outstretched, and managed to seize the retreating figure by the legs. This time both of them landed in a heap in the grass. Breathless but triumphant, Ben forced his opponent over onto his back.

"All right, I yield!" Tobias cried. "I pray you – let me alone!"

Ben's jaw dropped. He stared... Then, biting back words of reproach – not for his victim, but for himself – he loosened his grip on the beggar's shoulders, and got quickly to his feet.

Recovering his breath, he gazed downward. Even if the change in the other's voice had not given the game away, the woollen cap which had fallen off in the struggle would have done so. What it revealed was a swathe of jet-black hair, tied with a narrow ribbon which had come loose.

Ben was speechless. For he now found himself staring into a pair of luminous green eyes, beneath dark lashes. And as he watched, the girl who had called herself Tobias struggled up onto her elbows, and glared back at him.

"Well?" she demanded. "Now are you satisfied?"

Chapter Four

"I'm seldom lost for words, Ben," John Symes said sternly. "But now I believe I am. Just how did it happen, again?"

Ben explained, in less of a hurry this time. He told of his and Matt's encounter the evening before with Constable Plugg and "poor Tobias" – whose real name he had yet to learn. Then he recounted this morning's events, including his overpowering of the fugitive. After that, with people appearing in the Fields, Ben had feared the constable would be summoned, which meant that at the very least a flogging, or something more serious, awaited the beggar. To make matters worse, when she had got to her feet she was limping. So feeling somewhat ashamed, as well as responsible, Ben's only concern was to get her away. With the girl leaning on one arm, and Brutus's leash in his other hand, he had hurried them down the path to Bishopsgate Street, and home. Once in the house, both Ben and his companion had slumped exhaustedly upon the hallway floor. Only Brutus had seemed none the worse for his adventure, and had wandered off to find something to eat.

Having finished his tale, Ben waited. They stood in the Symes's kitchen, the girl seated nearby on a stool. John's eyes had wandered to the table, on which stood the two silver goblets stolen from the house by the Fields. Now he frowned at the raggedly dressed person before him.

"Could you get naught by begging?" he asked. "Did you have to stoop to thievery?"

There was no answer.

"Might we at least know your name?" John persisted.

Finally the girl spoke. "It's Jane – Jane Neale," she said in a sullen voice.

"And have you no family?"

She hesitated, whereupon Ben spoke up. "They

were killed in a house fire, with her the only survivor," he said. "At least, that's what she told the constable."

A defiant look came into the girl's eyes. "They may as well have been," she cried, "for we've lost everything!"

She turned to John. "What will you do with me?"

It was John's turn to hesitate. "I know what I *should* do," he said. "I should turn you over to a constable."

"But you won't."

Jane looked round sharply. She had not heard the street door open, as Ben had done, nor the soft footfalls in the passage. John's wife, Alice, stood in the doorway in her outdoor cloak, a basket on her arm. There was a snuffling from the corner as Brutus got up to greet her.

Alice eyed the ragged girl without any show of surprise. "That child looks half-starved," she said to John. "Have you asked her when she last ate anything?"

"Er...I was about to," John said stiffly.

Everyone looked at Jane. And suddenly, the girl's strength seemed to leave her. With a sigh, she bowed her head and put her face in her hands.

Alice set down her basket. "Stoke up the fire," she said to Ben, in a tone that made him jump to obey. "And fetch milk. I'll make porridge, then we'll find her something to wear. She looks about the same size as Kate."

She turned to her husband. "Unless that displeases you, sir?" she asked, her eyebrows raised.

John sighed, and shook his head.

That evening, after another performance at the Curtain, John and Ben returned home to find a stranger helping Kate and Meg set the table.

Thanks to the efforts of Alice Symes and her daughters, Jane had been transformed – from a ragged beggar into a well-groomed young girl. She had been washed, her face cleansed, her hair brushed and pinned up. She wore a plain blue gown of Kate's over a white kirtle, while on her feet were black shoes that, though somewhat worn, at least fitted her. Ben was relieved to see that her ankle, which she had hurt when she fell, seemed to be improving, for she hardly limped at all.

Kate and Meg were excited to have a guest for supper – especially one who had arrived in such dramatic fashion. As John walked in, the girls hurried to welcome him, but Jane held back with eyes lowered. Ben, she avoided looking at altogether. It was almost as if the events of the morning had never happened.

Feeling rather left out, Ben went off to wash. The truth was, he had thought of little else all day except his capture of Jane, as well as his rescue of her. Although on John's advice, he had said nothing to Lord Bonner's Men about the matter.

Today, supper was not the lively affair it usually was in the Symes household. After John had said grace and everyone began to eat, he and Alice talked of everyday matters, with Ben encouraged to join in. Luckily the rain had held off, and Lord Bonner's company had had a good audience, John said. Although some noisy gallants, sitting on the stage puffing pipes of tobacco, had made things difficult for the players. Gabriel Tucker had become so twitchy, it was all he could do to keep his temper and not threaten one man with his fist. However, he had got his own back later, Ben said, by accidentally knocking the fellow's hat off and stepping on it.

But only Meg laughed at the story, before falling silent. In fact, a silence soon settled over the whole table, and the reason was plain enough: Jane, who sat beside Ben, had not uttered a word throughout the meal.

When at last it was over, there was relief on every face. Kate and Meg went to help their mother, but as John rose, he caught Jane's eye.

"Will you come with Ben and me?" he asked, in a kindly enough tone. "It's time we had a proper talk."

The light was fading, and John lit a candle in the small chamber at the front of the house. The voices of passers-by could be heard outside – latecomers hurrying in and out of the city before the gates were closed. In the distance, the bells of Shoreditch sounded: the ringers of St Leonard's church were practising.

Motioning Jane to a bench, John sat down in the only chair. Ben took a stool near the latticed window.

"You may stay here tonight," John said. "You can share Kate and Meg's chamber."

Jane gave a nod. "Mistress Symes has told me already," she said quietly. "I'm grateful to you both."

"And to Master Button, I hope?" John glanced at Ben. "Or you could be spending the night in Bridewell, with a flogging awaiting you in the morning." He spoke of the place outside the city's west wall where vagrants were sent, which was little better than a prison.

For the first time Jane glanced at Ben. Then quickly she turned away.

"I've looked at those goblets you took," John went on. "They're of chased silver. Theft of anything worth more than a shilling is a felony – did you not know that?"

Jane bit her lip, but made no reply. Whereupon John added: "The penalty is imprisonment and branding – even death."

Again Jane said nothing, but Ben knew she was alarmed. She was no hardened villain, that much was clear. He guessed that John was only trying to shake her, by showing her the danger she faced. Ben was more intrigued than ever now to find out how such a girl came to be begging and stealing.

"So – I think it's best they are returned to the house they came from, before the owner returns and finds them gone," John said.

Jane looked up sharply. "Could that be done?"

"The matter's in hand," John told her. "Let's say I know someone who will find a way." Ben guessed that he meant Tom Slyte the rat-catcher. Tom knew everybody, including men who might take on such a task – by night, and for a price.

"Then you are most kind," Jane muttered, though to Ben's eyes she did not appear very grateful. He watched her as at last John asked how she came to be begging outside the theatre.

"For if I'm any judge of speech," John said, "you're not from London, nor anywhere near. Am I right?"

This time Jane answered promptly. "I said I hailed from the Midlands, and I spoke the truth," she said. "My family is from Shropshire, near the village of Coalbrookdale on the River Severn." She sniffed. "The name tells you all you need know, for it sits upon a bed of coal. Folk there talk of little else."

And all at once, as if sensing that both Ben and John would be good listeners, Jane seemed willing to talk.

"My father's a farmer," she said. "I mean, he was..." A frown creased her brow. "The farm's gone now, and he is dead. Indeed...it was the loss that killed him. He died of no sickness I know, save shame and heartbreak.

"And another thing I said is true," she went on. "We did lose everything, though not in a fire. I, my mother and my small brothers – even my grandmother, who's so old she can barely walk – we were thrown off our land. Land we had farmed for generations! Now they all live squeezed together in a tiny cottage that will likely fall down before the year is over!"

She paused, looking angry. And now, though Ben was wary of this girl, he no longer saw her as just a pitiful beggar. Instead he sensed the strength within her, along with the grief and hurt she carried. It was so fierce that it seemed to radiate from her, like the heat of Ned Campion's forge.

"But how could this be?" John asked. "If it was your family's farm as you say, and always had been, then how was it lost?"

For a while Jane gazed at the rush-strewn floor in silence, then looked up. "The Ironmaster wanted it," she said softly. "And whatever he wants, he will get."

The candle flame flickered, as if a breeze had disturbed it. Ben and his master exchanged looks, but the girl did not notice. Her eyes were on the rushes again.

"The Ironmaster?" John frowned. "Who is he?"

Jane seemed not to hear him. But as he was about to speak again, she answered calmly enough.

"He is a rich man – who means to become even richer. His appetite is vast: for land, for coal, and for iron. Indeed, for him the things are one and the same: for with more land, his men can dig more coal, and with more coal his workshop can smelt more iron."

She met John's eye. "It's a new method," she went on. "By using coal instead of charcoal in the furnaces, iron can be cast more easily, if you know how. Some men know – like The Ironmaster. And so, needing coal, he bought up the deeds to our farm – indeed, to all the farms nearby – and was able to force us off it. Simply because there is a great seam of coal beneath it!"

Then, to Ben and John's surprise, the girl sprang to her feet, fists clenched, and almost shouted the words at them.

"His name is Sir Miles Brandon," she cried, "and he's the reason I have spent weeks travelling across England, living any way I could, with rogues and beggars as my only friends: to seek him out, and pay him back in the manner he deserves!"

She gazed at them both, her eyes shining with anger. "And it may be that something I carry with me will help bring him to justice," she went on. "Then one beggar, at least, will have her revenge!"

Chapter Five

During the night Ben woke up on his pallet in the attic, thinking he had heard something. He listened, but the house was silent. Then he remembered all that had happened, and sat up. He wondered whether Jane was asleep in the girls' chamber below, or whether she too was lying awake. She was sorely troubled – but then who would not be, he thought, after what she had endured?

Little more was said after Jane had told her tale. The stolen goblets would be put back, under John's instruction. Meanwhile, he said, Jane could remain under their roof. Though from the looks John and Alice exchanged later, neither had much idea how they might help the girl.

What shocked them, as well as Ben, was Jane's accusation: that Sir Miles Brandon had forced her family off their farm, and thereby caused – in part at least – her father's death. For though no one spoke of it until Jane, Kate and Meg had gone to bed, the man was well known to all the players, as he was to the folk of Shoreditch and Hoxton.

Brandon was a nobleman, as clever as he was ruthless. A regular visitor to the court of Queen Elizabeth, he was involved in many areas of business: in wool and timber, as well as coal – and now, it seemed, in iron, too. He owned a mansion in Hart Street near the Tower of London, and had also built a big country house out at Hoxton. Here he held parties for important guests, at which London's players sometimes provided entertainment. Lord Bonner's Men had played at Brandon Court twice, though they received small reward for their services: food and drink, but little money. The truth was that Brandon was not liked: a greedy man, the players decided; always moving restlessly about, as if he would pounce on anything that caught his fancy. And now, Ben thought grimly, it seemed he had pounced upon

Farmer Neale's land in distant Shropshire, caring little how he took it. *The Ironmaster*, Jane had called him; and whatever The Ironmaster wanted, she said, he would get.

Sitting in the pitch darkness, Ben thought the matter over. Although Jane had lied to Constable Plugg, spinning her story of the fire and the deaths of her family, he knew it was but a tale to get charity, a speech taught to her by beggars; like the speeches Ben had to learn for performance. There was little doubt in his mind that the words she had spoken to him and John Symes this evening were the real truth. And now, as he had somehow known he would, he came to the decision that he would try to help her if he could. For it seemed to him that Jane had no one else to turn to in her quest for justice. Although how she might obtain that against a powerful man like Sir Miles Brandon was hard to imagine.

He lay back and pulled the coverlet to his chin. It was a challenge, and one in which he might fail. But at least, he thought sleepily, he would have tried... He closed his eyes, and the rain which had held off all day began to fall at last. Listening to it pattering on the thatch above his head, he fell into a deep sleep that lasted until dawn.

*

After Ben had taken Brutus out the next morning, he returned to the house to find Alice waiting. She was holding an old iron pot, one she sometimes used to boil broth in.

"I've an errand for you," she said. "Will you take this to Ned Campion, and ask him to mend the hole in it?"

Ben nodded, just as Jane appeared from the kitchen, wearing an old cloak of Kate's over her gown.

"You can take our guest with you," Alice added. "I've enough to do, without folk getting under my feet." *And keep out of trouble*, she seemed to say with her eyes: the meaning was clear enough. Ben took the pot, and with Jane following, went out again.

The rain had stopped early in the morning, but the road was still wet, with great puddles everywhere. Ben's shoes were already soaked from walking Brutus. Squelching, he led the way up Bishopsgate Street towards Shoreditch.

Jane kept her eyes on the way ahead, and seemed to have lapsed into one of her silences. It disappointed Ben, for he had questions he was keen to ask. Finally he opened his mouth – whereupon the girl spoke first.

"You think you're a hero, don't you?" she said in a cold voice.

Ben stopped.

"You were lucky, when you brought me down in the Fields," Jane went on, stopping to face him. "If I hadn't been trying to hold on to the silverware, you'd never have caught me." She gave a snort. "My littlest brother could outrun a town boy like you – and out-fight you too!"

"Town boy?" Ben was stung. "I'm not from any town. I'm from a village in Middlesex – and I've been helping out on farms ever since I could walk!"

But Jane pretended not to hear. Picking up her skirts, she marched off up the lane, not caring if she walked through puddles. Ben hurried to catch up.

"And I don't think I'm a hero," he went on as he drew alongside her. "I only did what I thought best. You saw what Constable Plugg's like – he'd have caught you easily, and sent you to Bridewell, as John said. Although he'd have given you a whipping himself first!"

Still Jane made no reply. The two of them walked side by side in silence, passing people in the street. Ahead, the church tower stood stark against the cloudy sky. Abruptly Jane stopped to gaze up at it.

"That's what I was told to look for," she murmured, as if to herself. "I saw it in the distance, when I first came..." She turned to Ben. "That's Shoreditch church, isn't it?"

Ben nodded. "St Leonard's."

"St Leonard's." There was a light in Jane's eye that Ben recognized: it was the way she had looked when she spoke of Sir Miles Brandon.

"A mile to the north-west is a big moated house, with gardens and a fountain," she said, as if remembering. "That's where The Ironmaster lives. There I will face him, and have my revenge!"

Ben stared at her. "You mean Brandon Court," he said. "It's Sir Miles's country house. He only comes here in the summer – that won't be for months."

"Then I'll wait," Jane told him. "He will come, sooner or later."

"You don't understand," Ben said, feeling quite alarmed. "Sir Miles Brandon is well known here, as he is in the city. He attends the Queen, and mixes with the highest nobles in England. He has servants and men-at-arms always at his side... You could never get near him, let alone gain entry to his house!"

Jane looked away. "It's none of your affair," she said. "Now, are we taking this old thing to the blacksmith's or not?"

Again she walked off. From Ned's forge came the familiar clang of hammer upon anvil. Clutching Alice's iron pot, Ben followed.

"Back again so soon?" Ned cried as they came in. "Not another tooth, is it?"

Ben shook his head, and held out the pot to show the hole. The smith glanced at it, then took it with a grunt. He looked busy today. While Squeaky Martin pumped the bellows for all he was worth, Ned dumped the pot on a bench by the wall.

"I fear this must wait, young Ben," he said, running a hand over his sweaty brow. "I've so much to do now, I scarce know which way to turn."

He waved a hand towards what looked like a heap of scrap iron in the corner. Ben saw knives, axes, smoothing irons, bedpans and cauldrons. None of those had been there during his painful visit two days ago.

"Who brought all that in, Master Ned?" he enquired. There looked to be more work for a blacksmith in that pile than the folk of Shoreditch gave Ned in a year.

"Well might you ask," Ned replied, with a grin beginning to spread. As the chief village gossip, and one who liked to be first with the news, he looked as if he had important tidings to impart. Ben waited.

"There's going to be a wedding," Ned announced. "That is, the wedding will be in London, but before that there's to be a great celebration – a betrothal party, at Brandon Court. For it's Sir Miles Brandon I speak of!" His grin broadened. "And every tradesman in Shoreditch is rubbing his hands at the business it will bring!"

Ben started at the mention of the very man he and Jane had been speaking of only minutes before. It seemed like an eerie coincidence. Glancing at Jane, who was standing by the doorway, he saw she was watching Ned with interest.

"Aye," the blacksmith went on, "they say the house is to be scoured, spruced and prettied from attic to cellar. New paintwork, new furniture, new plate – nothing will be overlooked!" He pointed to the heap of household goods. "Most of this came from the kitchens – I'm ordered to make good what I can, and what I can't repair I can have for scrap. Well, I said, it may be springtime, but thanks to Sir Miles, it's an autumn windfall for me!"

Ned broke into his donkey laugh, but Ben was still taking in the news. "Sir Miles?" he echoed. "You mean – he was here?"

"Course not – he's too high and mighty for that!" Ned retorted. "'Twas his steward, Nick Sparrow – remember him, do you, Whispering Nick?" When Ben nodded, the blacksmith went on: "Anyway, everything's got to be ready soon, the steward says, in time for the feasting and such when Sir Miles brings his betrothed to his house at Shoreditch." He sniffed. "Well – Hoxton, if you're particular. But 'tis a part of Shoreditch parish, is it not?"

But Ben's mind was racing. Sir Miles Brandon would be coming here after all – sooner that anyone expected.

"So...who is Sir Miles going to marry?" he asked.

"Ah – it gets better and better," Ned told him. "For she's a high-born maiden. She's Lady Imogen Walden – the daughter of old Lord Walden! What think ye of that?"

Ben had not heard of Lady Walden, but she sounded very important.

"Now, who's this you've brought along?" Ned asked. His interest had shifted to Jane. To Ben's surprise, she made a curtsy, and gave the blacksmith a sweet smile.

"I'm a friend to Mistress Symes, master," she said. "I'm honoured to meet you."

"Are you indeed?" Ned blinked. "Well, that's nobly said..." Then he looked round, for the bellows had stopped working. Squeaky Martin stood open-mouthed, staring at Jane as if she were some strange animal.

"Hey!" Ned shouted. "If I've told you once, I've told you a hundred times—"

Recovering quickly, Martin grabbed the bellows. The sound of air being pumped filled the forge once again.

"Ah well...you know I'm not one to stand and gossip, Master Ben," Ned said, evidently realizing he should get back to work. "That's the news. All of Shoreditch will be buzzing with it soon, if it's not already. A betrothal feast, eh? What with that, and the Whitsun Ale to follow, we'll have ourselves one long festival here, will we not?"

Then remembering Ben's reason for coming, he glanced at Alice's pot. "Will you tell Mistress Symes I'll do it as soon as I've got time? She'll understand."

With that he spat on his hands, seized his hammer and moved to his anvil. There was a dip worn in its surface, by many years of hard use. Upon it lay a pair of fire tongs, which Ned picked up and thrust into the furnace. The glow of hot coals grew fiercer, as Martin worked hard at the bellows.

Ben followed Jane out into the rain-washed air. Without a word, the two of them began to walk back along the street.

Suddenly, he realized that the notion he had last night of trying to help the girl was foolish. For one thing, she did not want his help – in fact, far from being grateful for his getting her to safety yesterday, she seemed almost to despise him for it. Yet when it suited her, she could turn on a winning smile, as she had done for Ned. And she had appeared so grateful to John and Alice, for giving her a roof... Now Ben felt as if he did not understand her at all. Could she really intend to get to Sir Miles Brandon somehow, and take revenge for what had befallen her family? Or was she, Ben began to think, so bound up in her rage and grief that she hardly knew what she did?

He glanced aside, thinking that really he knew very little of Jane. She was a contrary girl, he decided – but he could not help admiring her. She was very brave, to travel alone across England as she had done. And when he thought how close he had come to getting her caught for burglary, it shook him to the bone. But then he had also rescued Jane – which made him feel responsible for her, in a way.

Though quite what he could do for her now, he had no idea.

Chapter Six

*I*t was an hour later before Ben was able to tell John the news of Sir Miles Brandon's betrothal. The two of them spoke as they walked to the Curtain theatre. John had called a meeting of Lord Bonner's players that morning, to talk over some matters of importance.

"Well, that will set the cat among the pigeons," John murmured.

"I wanted to speak to you at the house, but Jane was nearby," Ben said. "The truth is, I fear she may do something desperate."

Quickly he told John all that Jane had said. When he had finished, his master, too, looked uneasy.

"I like it not, Ben. Though we may pity the girl in her plight, I think she brings trouble. I thought so from the moment she came into my house."

"What will you do?" Ben asked.

"I don't know yet," John told him. "Yet whatever Jane has done, I won't throw her out on the street. Alice would never forgive me." A thought struck him. "Perhaps I could find her a servant's place – for she seems in no hurry to return to her family."

That was true enough, Ben thought. They had walked into Holywell Lane now, with the Old Theatre and the Curtain towering before them on either side. There were people about: hirelings hoping for work, standing by the entrance to the Old Theatre. By the Curtain, only two people stood. Will Sanders was talking to another man... Then Ben saw a little tent, only half assembled, patterned with bright red and green squares – and his eyes widened. Beside him John groaned, as he too recognized the tiny theatre.

Sooner than expected, Harry Higgs and his puppets had arrived in Shoreditch.

*

Will was seething with anger.

"You talk to him," he said to John, as he and Ben walked up. "For if I listen to this fellow much longer, I can't answer for what might happen!" He turned to the puppet man, and pointed to his head. "And I haven't forgotten that lump I got last year – for which someone has yet to receive payment!"

Master Higgs merely grinned. And Ben, who had no real dislike for the man despite his crafty ways, looked him over with interest. He recognized the fellow's garish yellow doublet with its ribbons and bows, the striped breeches and the shoes with silver buckles. His beard was cut short, but his black moustache was grown to a splendid length, its ends curled upwards like a dagger's hilt. His puppet booth was a three-sided tent, with an opening at the front covered by a curved roof. The operator would sit inside, concealed beneath the little stage, and work the puppets above his head. Nearby was a large wicker basket, containing Higgs's possessions. Some way off, the old mule by which he travelled about the country was quietly cropping the grass.

"Master Symes!" Harry Higgs swept off his hat with a grand gesture. His other hand he kept hidden inside his doublet, as if he had a weapon concealed – which, Ben thought, he might well have.

"And is this Master Button?" the puppet master asked cheerfully. His sharp little eyes met Ben's. "You've grown, young fellow. You'll be a handsome youth one day. Too old for skirts by then, eh?"

He laughed, showing gaps in his teeth. Ben nodded politely, wondering how John would deal with the man. For in truth, the lane by the theatres was common ground, for anyone to use. There was no law by which the players could force the puppet master to leave.

"Master Higgs..." John looked the man in the eye. "We did not expect you before Whitsun. Do you mean to waylay our theatregoers again, with your little company?"

"Fair competition's no crime," Higgs said, putting his hat back on. Then, with a flourish which startled the three players, he brought his hand out of his clothing with a glove puppet on it. It was a green dragon with wooden teeth and red beads for eyes, its jaws worked by the puppet master's fingers and thumb.

"Who's this scurvy lot?" the dragon said – or rather, Master Higgs said it in a gruff tone, one of many voices he used for his characters. "Tell 'em to take themselves off, or I'll breathe fire and scorch their breeches!"

"Now, now – that's not very polite." Higgs wagged a finger at the dragon. "These good folk are servants to the noble Lord Bonner. Some say they're the best company about London – but then others favour the Lord Chamberlain's Men..." Higgs put on a sad smile, and faced the players. "A man must shift for himself in this world, my friends. Is it not so?"

There was a creak, and the heavy doors of the Curtain swung open. Solomon Tree appeared, to gaze gloomily at them all. "Rain later," he said. "We may have to cancel..." His eye fell on Higgs. "What's he doing here?"

"Here's another of 'em!" the dragon cried. "This one's got a face as long as a horse!"

Higgs made a *tut-tut* sound at his puppet, and was about to speak, but Solomon was quicker.

"Is that a frog?" he enquired, blank-faced. "He'll need water... Hold on, while I fetch a pail."

"Frog!" The dragon bared its teeth at the lanky comic. "Take that back, you long streak of bacon, or I'll singe your beard!"

Will Sanders could stand it no longer. His hand shot out to grab hold of the dragon. "Not if I break your neck first you won't," he cried. "And your master's arm with it!" He was glaring at Harry Higgs, who tensed as the fist closed about his arm.

But John Symes put a hand on Will's shoulder. "Enough," he said firmly.

Will let go, and turned away with a muffled oath.

"We want no trouble," John said to the puppet master. "But I told you last year, we don't take kindly to you setting up right next to the theatre. So – can't we come to an arrangement of some kind?"

But Higgs was angry. He took off the glove puppet and massaged his wrist, with a glare at Will. "I'll make no arrangement with ruffians," he muttered. "And as I told *you*, John Symes – fair competition is no crime."

He moved to his hamper and threw the lid open. He laid the dragon puppet inside, then began whistling to himself as he searched for something. He behaved as if the players were no longer there.

The others glanced at John, who shook his head. Shoving the doors wide, he walked into the Curtain yard. Will and Solomon followed, with Ben behind. As he entered the theatre, he threw a last glance at the puppet master. Higgs's back was to him, but Ben's sharp eyes noticed a stiffness in the man's limbs that he had not seen before. As he watched, Higgs stood up, arched his back and put a hand to it, as if it pained him.

Even puppet masters, Ben thought sadly, had to grow old.

*

John faced the company, who stood about the theatre yard. Ben sat with Matt on the front of the stage, listening closely, for the news was not good. It seemed the Lord Chamberlain's Men were soon to put on one of their most popular plays – written, of course, by Master Shakespeare.

"It's *The Comedy of Errors*," John said. "It always pulls the crowds in. So what with that, and Higgs's puppets outside our door, we must do some hard thinking."

"I've done some already," Solomon said. "If Higgs won't go of his own accord, I think we should help him on his way, with a few shillings for his pains."

"Agreed!" Gabriel Tucker cried fiercely. "And if someone will hold him down, I volunteer to tie the knave to that mangy mule of his and lead him away, by whatever road you like!"

"We'll do no such thing, Master Gabriel," John said. "A brabble between us and Higgs is just the excuse James Plugg needs to make trouble for us." He frowned at Ben and Matt. "And I don't want to hear of our prentices mocking the constable again, and stirring up his wrath."

The boy players exchanged looks.

Handsome Hugh Cotton, who had been standing

in front of the stage, now spoke up. "I thought we had no fear of puppets," he said with a smile. "If it's fair competition the fellow wants, let him have it – and the same goes for the Lord Chamberlain's Men. We could play *The Witch of Wandsworth* – that always shows us at our best. We can put bills out: *As played before the Queen's Majesty at Whitehall*. Everyone knows what a success that was."

"The play's too recent," John objected. "All of London has seen it. A revival so soon wouldn't fill the theatre."

There were disappointed looks, whereupon Will coughed to get everyone's attention. "There's, er, something I've thought on," he said to John. "I suppose you've heard the talk around Shoreditch, about Sir Miles Brandon getting betrothed, and having a feast and everything?" When John gave a nod he went on: "He'll be wanting entertainment, won't he? And if we get our name in before the Chamberlain's Men do...well, Sir Miles might want to impress his bride-to-be by showing how generous he is for once." He shrugged. "Higgs can't follow us into Brandon Court, can he?"

There was a moment – then smiles broke out.

"A splendid notion!" Hugh exclaimed. "And could Lord Bonner not put a good word in for us?" He looked at John. "He sees Sir Miles at court sometimes, doesn't he?"

"I believe so – and if a message were sent, asking him to act quickly..." John, too, was grinning. "When I think upon those who'll be invited to the festivities – earls and knights, and Brandon's rich merchant friends – we may find ourselves invited to perform elsewhere. Why, we could pick and choose where we go all summer!"

There were cries of approval from the whole company. Though no one had any liking for Sir Miles Brandon, a performance at his betrothal feast would be the best showcase Lord Bonner's Men could have since they played before the Queen. Now everyone was talking at once. And Will Sanders, seldom one to have a bright idea, found himself being patted on the back.

Matt turned to Ben. "Well, that's lifted everyone's spirits," he said.

But Ben was looking at John, and wondered if his master had forgotten what he had said earlier: how, for a certain Mistress Jane, the arrival of Sir Miles Brandon would put the cat among the pigeons.

So it would, Ben thought. For if Lord Bonner's Men were invited to Brandon Court, the talk in the Symes household would be of little else in the days leading up to their performance. Sir Miles's name would be on everyone's lips – if it wasn't already.

How Jane would take the news, he did not know. But it seemed to him that someone would have to keep a close eye on her from now on, lest she did something terrible – something which could lead not just to a flogging, but to Tyburn: a place by the western road out of London, where stood the most famous gallows in England.

Chapter Seven

After their performance that day, Ben and Matt came out of the theatre to find a small but lively crowd, mostly children, on the other side of Holywell Lane. They soon saw why the group had gathered: Harry Higgs had moved his tent to a better spot, closer to the Old Theatre.

"I suppose he thinks the Chamberlain's Men will get a better audience than us," Matt remarked dryly. "Shall we go and bother the old rogue?"

But Ben gave a start: on the edge of the group were Kate and Meg Symes – and beside them stood Jane.

Quickly he crossed the lane and walked towards them. Matt followed.

"Ben!" Meg greeted him with a smile. "Look – it's *Gawain and the Green Knight*!" Then, seeing his face, her smile faded.

"Does Alice know you're here?" Ben asked – then he glanced at Jane. "She doesn't, does she?"

"Oh, Ben – you won't tell, will you?" Meg said. Behind her the crowd shouted with laughter at the antics of Higgs's puppets. "We'll be back home before Mother – she's gone to the lacemaker's."

Kate, always the practical one, spoke up. "Meg wanted so much to go," she said. "All her friends are here. It can't do any harm, can it? Mother and Father need not find out."

"What if they do?" Jane was staring defiantly at Ben. "I'll go wherever I like," she told him. "If Kate and Meg want to tag along, who am I to stop them?"

Already Meg had turned back to watch the puppets. A cheer rose, and from the applause it was clear the performance was over. Ben's eyes strayed towards the little tent, to see Master Higgs emerge from behind it with a puppet on each hand, to take his bow.

"They'll see the show anyway, at the Whitsun Ale," Ben told Jane. "But here, the puppet master's our rival. He's a sly rogue, who takes our audience—"

"Oh, stuff and stale!" Jane retorted. "You get hundreds of people in your theatre. How many are here – maybe forty or fifty?"

"Alice will be worried if she comes home and finds Kate and Meg gone, without knowing where," Ben insisted, his temper rising in the face of Jane's stubbornness.

Jane glared at him. Seeing them both getting angry, Kate was about to try and calm things, when Matt spoke up from behind.

"Is this a family squabble, or can anyone join in?" he asked in his innocent voice.

Kate smiled: since the winter Matt had become a friend to them all. "I hope you gave a good performance today, Master Fields," she said.

"I always do," Matt replied – then his gaze strayed to Jane. "And who's this?"

"Look – we can't stay." Ben nodded towards the Curtain. The audience had gone, and some of the players were now emerging from the doors. "Your father will be coming out at any moment."

At that Meg looked uneasy, but Kate acted swiftly. With a brief goodbye to Matt, she took her sister's hand and pulled her away. As they hurried across the Fields, Meg glanced back at Jane, but the girl shook her head. Soon, to Ben's relief, the two were far enough away not to be recognized. They would be home within minutes.

There was a silence as Ben, Matt and the person they had both encountered three days back in her guise as Tobias eyed each other. "Well now..." Matt raised his eyebrows at Ben. "Will you not present me to your friend?"

But Jane answered at once. "I'm not his friend," she said. "I'm visiting Mistress Symes...though I may not be staying much longer." Then, with a frosty glance at Ben, she turned on her heel and walked off.

The boys watched her go. It was clear that Matt had not recognized Jane from his previous sight of her, when he had played his trick on Constable Plugg. But then, Ben thought, when he first came home to find her looking as she did now, he had barely recognized her himself.

"She's a strange one, isn't she?" Matt said. "You never told me John and Alice had a guest."

"I must have forgotten." Ben was now watching Master Higgs hurry round with his hat before the crowd broke up. A few people dropped pennies and halfpennies in.

"Well, that's no surprise," Matt said. "It looks to me as if your mind's been elsewhere of late. Not in trouble, are you?"

"Trouble?" Ben echoed. "Of course not – why should I be?" Raising a hand, he began to move off. "I'll see you tomorrow," he said – whereupon the other burst into laughter.

"What did I say about you being absent-minded?" Matt cried. "There's the proof! Why would I see you tomorrow, when there's no performance? It's Sunday, woolly-brain!"

And with that Matt walked off, still laughing to himself.

Ben watched him go, feeling a fool. He wasn't usually absent-minded. It was all Jane's fault, he thought crossly. If she hadn't annoyed him again... Then, with a sigh, he too began to make his way home.

The morrow may have been Sunday, but it turned out to be more eventful than Ben expected.

The skies had cleared, and it was a fine morning. Along with his master and the rest of the Symes family, Ben walked down to the church of St Botolph's, near Bishopsgate. Hog Lane, where they lived, was closer to here than to St Leonard's, and the Symes's belonged to St Botolph's parish. All citizens were expected to attend their parish church every week. Those who didn't go might be suspected of being Catholics, and could be fined – which was why Jane found herself being taken unwillingly to the service. She did not hide her relief when they came out into the sunshine again and began walking homewards along the busy street.

Ben had not forgotten what Jane had said the day before: that she might not be staying at the Symes's much longer. He wondered what she meant by it. In fact, the longer he spent with the girl, he realized, the less he seemed to know her – which to his mind, made no sense at all.

John and Alice walked in front, dressed in their Sabbath clothes. John wore a black doublet and breeches, though his hat with the blue jay's feather was somewhat garish: it always marked him out as one of the theatre folk, Alice said. She herself wore a black gown, and the girls were similarly dressed. Jane, wearing one of Kate's gowns, lagged behind the others.

All at once, Ben's ears pricked up. For a while he had been aware of a noise from behind, from the direction of the city. Now he heard hoof-beats, and a loud voice ordering folk to make way. He turned, as the others did, to see a large body of riders coming towards them. He caught the glint of sunlight on polished horse-trappings, and the flash of bright colours. All along the street, people stood back to let the procession pass. Excited talk broke out, some saying it must be an earl or another important person leaving London with his train. Could it even be the Queen herself?

Then, as the horsemen drew nearer, there were murmurs of recognition...and the same name rose from a dozen mouths: "It's Brandon! Sir Miles Brandon's come to Shoreditch!"

Ben stiffened, thinking at once of Jane's talk of revenge – against the very man who was about to pass by within a few feet of her! Worried now, he stood beside Meg, who was of course delighted by the spectacle. On his other side, Jane was craning her neck to see. But Ben realized he had no time to act in any case, for already the riders were abreast of them. He could only watch as the column thundered past.

At its head were a dozen attendants riding in pairs, dressed in Brandon's green and gold livery. Only certain noblemen were allowed to keep liveried servants – a special licence had to be got from the Queen for that. The men carried small round shields known as bucklers, and looked ready to push people aside if they had to. Behind them, riding on his own, came an old man in a black gown. White-haired and hunched over the reins, he ignored the bystanders. Ben recognized him at once: Nicholas Sparrow, Sir Miles's steward, whom villagers like Ned Campion called "Whispering Nick" because of his soft voice.

But it was the next man who caught everyone's eye. Even if he had not been sitting astride a splendid Barbary horse, it was obvious that he was the most important person in the procession. Along with everyone else, Ben gazed up at the figure of Sir Miles Brandon. Some women made curtsies as he approached, while men took off their hats.

There was no mistaking him: Ben remembered the sharp eyes, the broad face and the neat blond beard, as well as the many rings upon the man's fingers. Brandon wore well-cut riding clothes, and finely tooled boots of oxhide. On his head was a black velvet hat, worn to one side, trimmed with gold lace and sprouting a peacock's feather. A sword with a jewelled hilt hung at his hip, while his harness sparkled with silver mountings. Behind him rode more attendants in livery, and behind them came yet more servants, but on foot and in plain workaday clothes. These men led packhorses, heavily laden with chests and boxes. And if there were any watchers who had not yet learned of Sir Miles's betrothal and the forthcoming feast, they soon heard the news. It seemed the master of Brandon Court had arrived ahead of his bride-to-be to make everything ready.

As the nobleman passed, Ben looked sharply at Jane – but the girl never moved. Nor did she show any sign of anger. Sir Miles swept by on his fine horse, acknowledging the crowds with a wave, but she merely gazed until he was out of sight. Packhorses were soon trotting by, snorting and straining under their loads. Finally the last was gone, and people began talking excitedly.

The first of the Symeses to speak was the youngest. "Did you see the jewels, and the silver?" Meg cried. "It was like the Queen's train – though without the coach, I mean. Even the attendants looked like lords!"

"Not like lords," her father said quietly. "They looked like soldiers to me – a private army."

Ben knew that John was right. Though it was common for men of high station to ride about with many servants, even a hundred or more, Brandon's men were a hard-faced lot. The family watched in silence as the procession disappeared in clouds of dust.

But for Ben and his master, the day's events were far from over. That same afternoon, a messenger on horseback arrived at the house in Hog Lane, causing Brutus to bark furiously and sending Meg into another flurry of excitement. But now she had good reason – for the news was indeed important:

Master John Symes, the leading player of Lord Bonner's Men, was to come to Brandon Court after sunset and attend Sir Miles. He was permitted to bring one other person with him, but no more. And standing in the passage listening, Ben, too, felt a pang of excitement.

Surely, as John's prentice, he would be the one to go?

Chapter Eight

Some hours later, taking turns to carry a blazing torch, Ben and John walked through Finsbury Fields in the dusk. Ben's hopes had been fulfilled: he was to accompany his master to Brandon Court. He felt excited – and a little nervous, too.

They passed the windmills, their sails motionless. Before them was the lane to Hoxton, just visible in the gloom. Then they were soon in open meadow, with only darkness before them. A barn owl flew silently overhead.

The ground was rougher now, with watery ditches

and small hillocks. They were glad of the torch, for the lights of Shoreditch had faded behind. Hoxton was due north, a tiny hamlet of a dozen houses, but their way led north-west, where Brandon Court stood on its own. At first they could see nothing, until a pinpoint of light appeared in the distance. As they drew nearer, it separated into two lights, which a few minutes later became flaming brands fixed to stone gateposts. Walls stretched away on either side, while above them rose the familiar bulk of the great house. A gravelled lane led to the gates, in front of which was a wooden bridge over the moat. Although moated castles were a relic of bygone days in England, some rich men had trenches dug about their country manors, either from mere fancy, or to make them more private. It was well known that Sir Miles was suspicious of intruders: Ben remembered the watchful servingmen who had stood about the hall when Lord Bonner's Men had last performed here, as if to remind them they were mere players and not to be trusted.

There was a guard on the gate, who was expecting them. He took their torch, then pointed to an entrance across a courtyard, where another torch blazed. Lights showed at a few windows, and horses could be heard somewhere, snickering in their stables. John and Ben entered the house, and followed a wide passage which ended at a stout oak door. Here another guard led them into a dimly lit, panelled chamber, smaller than Ben expected.

"You'd think we were being admitted to the Queen's presence," John muttered as they stepped into the room – then halted, and quickly made his bow. Ben did the same, and straightened up to see Sir Miles Brandon seated at a table, eyeing them both.

"Master Symes – I remember you," the knight said, and waved them forward with his bejewelled hand. He raised an eyebrow at Ben, whereupon John presented his prentice, Master Button.

Brandon's hard little eyes fixed upon John. "I'll engage you once again to play for me," he said, "but make no mistake: my first choice would be the Lord Chamberlain's Men. Think of this as a favour to your patron, the noble Lord Bonner. I expect you to honour him."

Now his gaze fell upon Ben. "I hope your boys know how to conduct themselves," he said to John. "I want no roughness in your performance – my bride-to-be is a lady of taste and breeding. Her father, Lord Walden, and others of the highest rank will be among my guests. Is that clear?"

John managed a polite nod. "We thought to play *The Old Wives' Tale* for your pleasure, sir," he replied.

"It's a witty piece by Master Peele, a poet who has written royal pageants—"

"I know who he is," Brandon said shortly. "I leave the choice of play to you." Suddenly the man got to his feet and, picking up a goblet of fine Italian glass, took a drink. "More important than the play, in any case," he went on, "are your musical skills. You'll not perform in my hall this time – a great pavilion is being put up in the gardens. My steward will see you bestowed there, on the day."

He glanced aside, and Ben and John realized there was someone else seated at the table, half in shadow. "Whispering Nick" Sparrow was surveying the two players with hooded eyes, like a sleepy hawk. He too had a goblet before him, from which he took a sip before he spoke. And as most people did, Ben and his master strained to hear the man's voice.

"Friday next," Sparrow wheezed at them. "I expect you in the morning at ten of the clock. I myself will hear you rehearse. You'll perform from noon until night – likely until dawn, in fact, so you must be alert. Nothing shall be left to chance – we look to you for the very best entertainment." He frowned. "You should thank Sir Miles for his generosity in hiring you!"

Beside Ben, John stiffened. "Our company will not disappoint, Master Sparrow," he said. "We played before the Queen at Whitehall last Christmas—"

"Yes, yes…" Sir Miles interrupted him impatiently. "Give of your best, and I'll reward you well." He looked at Sparrow. "What think you, master steward – three angels?"

"It sounds more than enough, sir," Whispering Nick replied.

Ben glanced at his master. Three angels amounted to only twenty shillings. With the regular players and boys, along with hired men and musicians, there might be twenty performers – which meant less than a shilling each after expenses. The players earned at least a shilling for an afternoon's work at the Curtain – while Sir Miles expected them to work longer, for a smaller fee. John cleared his throat and began to explain – but again Sir Miles broke in irritably.

"Very well – spare me your wheedling. Five angels, and that's as high as I'll go!"

Realizing this was the best bargain he would get, John nodded. "On behalf of our company, sir, I thank you."

"So you should," Sparrow muttered. "For there'll be food and drink prepared by the finest cooks in London. You'll eat better than you've done in months!"

There was a silence, from which it was clear that the meeting was over. John and Ben made their bows, but Sir Miles merely snapped an order over his shoulder. Only now did the man-at-arms, who had concealed himself in shadow by the wall, step forward to usher them out.

Once away from Sir Miles's presence, Ben found himself thinking of Jane's account of the man she called The Ironmaster. He recalled the glint in her eyes in the front parlour that day she first came to the Symes's house. And here was the man on whom she planned to take revenge?

If ever a task looked hopeless, Ben thought, this was surely it.

"Friday," Handsome Hugh said. "That gives us time to be ready."

Solomon Tree was shaking his head. "Five angels," he muttered. "Why is it that the richest men are always the worst misers?" He turned to John Symes. "I need a new calfskin for my drum. That's my wage for the day..."

"I'll buy you one," John replied patiently. "Now, can we speak of other matters?" He looked round the Curtain yard at the rest of the company. "It seems Sir Miles requires our services more as a consort of music than as players," he went on. "So we'll give them *The*

Old Wives' Tale first, then seat ourselves to play for the dancing. It will be a long evening – and a long night. And mindful of Solomon's words, we'll use the minimum of hired men – those who play instruments." He nodded towards Hugh and Gabriel. "We've two recorders, along with my lute, and Solomon's drum—"

"And my hautboy," Matt put in cheerfully. "That's an orchestra already."

There was laughter. Matt was struggling with the hautboy, a reed instrument which was hard to learn. Even Solomon smiled, for the company were in good humour. It was Monday morning, another clear day, and they all looked forward to playing at Brandon Court before so many distinguished guests. The prospect of free food and drink helped to make up for the modest payment. Ben, standing beside Matt, wondered if he would get to play the lute too, even though he was still having lessons. To his relief, John threw him a smile.

"Fear not – we'll find work for both you boys," he said. "No one will be left out."

The yard doors opened and Will Sanders appeared. Quickly he went over to speak with John – and somehow, Ben knew it was bad news. The next moment, John called him over.

"I'm going back to the house," he said, with a frown. "Alice has sent word – it seems our guest has flown."

For a moment Ben did not understand.

"I mean Jane," John said. "She's gone!"

The company rehearsed all morning, but Ben found it hard to keep his mind on his work. Instead, he thought about Jane. The girl was abed when he and John had returned the previous night, and had been out with Kate on an errand when they left the house this morning. Now, questions crowded his head: where had Jane gone? And most alarming – now that she knew Sir Miles was close by, what did she intend to do?

It was noon before John returned. Then, as the company stopped work to take their dinner, Ben at last learned what had happened.

"She's a sly young wench," John said, with a shake of his head. "She made use of my roof – and of Alice's soft heart – for as long as she needed, then took off without a word!"

Quickly he told Ben the tale. Jane had gone with Kate to the bakehouse in Shoreditch – but after paying the baker, Kate turned round to find Jane had vanished. She looked for her in the street, but there was no sign of the girl. When Kate returned home and told her mother, it soon became obvious that Jane had planned her flight carefully.

"Her beggar boy's clothes, which she kept in a bundle by her bed, are gone," John said. "She must have been wearing them under Kate's gown – which she's now stolen!"

It was rare for John to be angry, but Ben understood why he was now. Jane had taken advantage of his whole family, who had made her welcome, and repaid their kindness with deceit. John had even saved the girl from arrest, by getting the goblets she'd stolen returned. Now, recalling what she said at the puppet show about not staying much longer, Ben felt a stab of guilt. He knew he should have told John – but not wanting to tell tales on Kate and Meg, he had kept quiet. So in a way, he too was deceiving John and Alice – something he had never done. Now it seemed John was right all along: Jane had brought nothing but trouble.

"She knew when to go," John went on, "for if she'd tried to leave during the night, Brutus would have barked and woken us up. This way, she could disappear among the folk in the street." He sighed. "Kate and Meg are upset, for they thought Jane was their friend. As for me...well, now I think it may be for the best, in a way. I did not know how to help the girl, save by finding her a servant's place. Yet I'm troubled..." He met Ben's eye. "And I think you can guess why."

"Sir Miles Brandon." Ben nodded. "I watched her yesterday when he passed us in Bishopsgate Street – she never took her eyes off him."

"Well, whatever she has in mind," John said, "she'll not get inside Brandon Court. The place is guarded like a fortress." He sighed. "I wouldn't report her to Plugg – I mean for the theft of Kate's clothes, or even those goblets. Jane wasn't much good either as a beggar or a thief, was she? Now, unless she teams up with others soon, she's alone, and unused to city ways. She could find herself in all sorts of danger."

Ben was thoughtful. Remembering the kick Jane gave him when he tried to catch her, it seemed to him she might be able to look after herself better than John imagined.

"Well – there's an end to it," John said, and clapped him on the shoulder. "I'm relieved she's gone, for we've enough to busy ourselves with." He managed a smile. "If you practise hard from now until Friday, it's my belief you can learn the lute part to four or five of Master Dowland's Airs – what do you say?

"Are you in earnest?" Ben asked. He was dismayed: Master Dowland was a celebrated lute-player and composer, whose book of songs was hugely popular. But many of his pieces were also hugely difficult.

"When am I not in earnest?" John asked him. "You're a fast learner, and you have nimble fingers. See how many you can master in time for our performance – but be prepared for a sore thumb! Now, I've a powerful appetite…shall we get something to eat?"

Ben nodded and followed John out, thinking how much things had changed in the space of but an hour.

And by the time he stepped out onto the Curtain stage that afternoon, he had managed to put Jane out of his mind. Instead, he was facing a different sort of problem: how to learn four tunes for the lute in as many days!

Chapter Nine

Friday morning, the day of Sir Miles's betrothal feast, brought a blue sky with fleecy white clouds and a gentle breeze. And soon after ten of the clock, Lord Bonner's Men crossed the wooden bridge to present themselves at the gates of Brandon Court.

It had been one of the busiest weeks Ben could remember. With practising his lute every day, rehearsing each morning with the company, and performing in the afternoons, he was so tired at night he fell asleep the moment he lay his head down. But as the days passed, his excitement grew, as the company got ready for the festivities. Even Harry Higgs failed to dampen their spirits, although the puppet master was still outside the Curtain most days, taking a slice of their audience. On Thursday, however, he did not appear, and the players' hopes rose that he had taken himself off.

For Ben, Jane's stay at the Symes house was but a memory now. Today he stood in the sunshine with Matt, waiting for the gates of Brandon Court to open, without a thought of the girl in his head.

Including the hired men there were sixteen players, along with a cart carrying their props, costumes and instruments. The cart was drawn by Ben's friend, the old horse Tarlton. Tarlton was looked after by Will Sanders, who stabled him at the White Hart Inn by Bishopsgate.

"He has an easy life," Will was saying. "A warm bed, hay and bran...it'll do him good when summer comes and we go touring. Then he can earn his keep, and shed some of that weight he's put on."

"Talking of putting on weight..." Hugh poked Will in the stomach. "Your jerkin's looking a bit tight, isn't it?"

Will scowled, but the others laughed. Ben had been looking down at the moat, wondering how deep it was. His gaze wandered to the high brick wall that surrounded the house and gardens. Over the wall he could see the top of a huge tent, brightly painted in green and gold – the colours of Sir Miles's livery. A flag flew from a pole, displaying the Brandon crest. Now voices could be heard, followed by the sound of a bar sliding back. As the gates opened, a guard bade the players enter. So with Will leading Tarlton behind, Lord Bonner's players walked into Brandon Court – to gaze at the splendid sight.

The gardens that Ben had last glimpsed by night had been transformed. The great pavilion of painted sailcloth, with pennants fluttering in the breeze, almost covered the newly scythed grass. Nearby was a banqueting house made of poles and green foliage. Sir Miles's gardeners had gathered what spring flowers they could: daffodils, primrose and celandine were everywhere, along with ribbons and hangings to add more colour. Gravelled walks between raised flower beds led towards Sir Miles's fountain, the wonder of Hoxton, which needed a gardener's boy to work the pump or it would not flow. Between the gardens and the house, servants were carrying tables and stools. A stage of boards set upon trestles could be seen inside the pavilion, one side of which was open.

Matt stared in amazement. "All this to mark a

promise of marriage?" he said. "I wonder what the wedding will be like."

"The wedding feast will be at Sir Miles's town house," John said, "after the church ceremony. If I'm any judge, it'll last for days. This is just a taste of it, to show off Brandon's wealth to everyone – especially his bride's father, Lord Walden." He shrugged. "Marriages between nobles are always arranged – it's like a business matter."

"And they're welcome to it!" Gabriel Tucker said stoutly. "I grew up in a poor family, but my father let my sisters choose their own husbands. He'd never have forced them to marry against their wishes!" He glared round at everyone. "From what I've heard, Lady Imogen Walden's but a maid of seventeen years, while Brandon's thirty if he's a day. If she had any choice, would she truly pick a man like him?"

"The lives of such folk are not like ours, Master Gabriel," John said mildly. "She's been brought up to obey her father – and she has but a modest dowry. Lord Walden may be a nobleman, yet his fortune's naught compared to that of Sir Miles. But in any case, why dwell on it? We're players for hire, are we not?"

"And here's our Master of Revels for the day," Solomon grunted. "Sparkling Sparrow!"

The others hid smiles at the sight of Whispering Nick shuffling towards them, leaning on his steward's staff. With his black gown and old-fashioned cloth hat, he looked as if he were organizing a funeral rather than a betrothal feast.

"You're late," were his first words. "Get yourselves into the pavilion, then show me the first act of your play. I can judge what pleases Sir Miles – he's not a man to suffer fools."

Some of the players frowned. Lord Bonner's Men were accounted one of the finest companies in England...and sensing their mood, John spoke up. "If you'll give us half an hour, we'll be ready," he said. "I told you: Bonner's Men do not disappoint."

"I hope not," Sparrow said hoarsely. As he walked off, he called over his shoulder. "Half an hour and no more!"

Solomon watched him go. "I don't suffer fools either," he said. "But for him, I could make allowances."

There were chuckles, and the tension eased. Will clicked his tongue at Tarlton and led him off. The others followed, Matt walking at Ben's side.

"How are your fingers?" he asked.

"Sore," Ben said, and showed him. "John made me practise till they bled."

"My mother made me play the hautboy every night, until I was so short of breath I thought I was dying," Matt said. "If I faint and topple off the stage, you'll know why."

Ben put on an innocent expression. "How will we know it's not another of your fake fits?"

Matt grinned. "I was rather good that day, wasn't I?" he said.

By mid-afternoon, however, the company's enthusiasm had ebbed away – for the performance of *The Old Wives' Tale* was little more than a waste of time. Their rehearsal had been cut short after Master Sparrow gave his grudging approval. People were arriving, and the steward had to hurry off to attend them. Already the gardens were full of chatter and laughter – and it seemed Sir Miles's guests preferred to stay outside, enjoying the sunshine. They wandered in and out of the banqueting house and the pavilion, but few bothered to watch the play. So with some relief, Lord Bonner's Men at last took their bows to a handful of people, mostly servants who had sneaked in. Then the players changed behind the curtain that formed a makeshift tiring room, and went outside.

Though Ben and Matt were used to playing before

people of every sort, even nobles of the Queen's court, they were subdued by the splendour on display. Men in richly embroidered clothes, some with gold chains on their chests, strutted about with ladies of fashion in silk gowns, shining with jewels. Servants attended them with trays of silver goblets, trying to avoid the small dogs which ran about. But the centre of attention was a slender, auburn-haired young woman in a gown of eggshell blue: Lady Imogen Walden. Sir Miles, in a splendid red and gold doublet, was often at her side, but was sometimes distracted by men eager to speak with him. Always close to the lady, however, was a grey-haired man in a sober black gown, whom Ben guessed was her father. That was confirmed when, to their surprise, Lord Walden took time to speak to the players.

Bonner's Men were hungry and thirsty, but they were not permitted to enter the banqueting tent, where rich dainties were laid out on tables spread with fine carpets. Instead, a few dishes had been set aside for them on a trestle nearby, which was in any case more to their liking. They were eating and chattering in their usual manner, when John Symes called for quiet. The others turned and made their bows as Lord Walden approached, flanked by two servants. But at sight of his smile, they began to relax.

"Well done, masters," His Lordship said. "A delightful play... I'm sorry you did not have a better audience for it."

"No matter, My Lord..." John returned the man's smile. "It's our pleasure to perform. We wish your daughter Lady Imogen a happy marriage, and a long life."

Lord Walden nodded. "I'm acquainted with your noble patron," he said. "It's a pity he is not here today."

"I'm sure he regrets it, sir," John said. "He's at his country house. It's a long way..." He trailed off, somewhat embarrassed – and the players knew why. John had once told them, in confidence, that Lord Bonner disliked Sir Miles Brandon as much as they did. Ben leaned close to Matt.

"I'll bet he's made some excuse not to come," he whispered. Matt nodded.

Watching Lord Walden, Ben sensed a sadness behind the man's soft grey eyes. With a farewell nod, the old man turned and walked away, his servants following.

"He's one of the Queen's most trusted councillors, did you know that?" one of the hired men murmured.

"And that's the chief reason for the marriage,"

Gabriel said. "Sir Miles spends all this money so that he can marry into a powerful family with more influence at Court than he has."

"That may be," Hugh said quietly. "But I wager there isn't a man here who isn't smitten by Lady Imogen. Most would walk through flames to win her hand."

There was silence – then the players burst into laughter.

"Why, he's in love!" Gabriel cried. "I knew there was something wrong with him!"

"That's why he nearly forgot that last speech," Matt said. "One glimpse of Her Ladyship and he was struck dumb!"

"Dazzled, more like," Solomon put in gloomily. "There's so much gold and silver out there, my eyes are hurting."

"Don't be hard on Master Hugh," the hired man said, with a smile. "A man in love is to be pitied – 'tis an affliction."

"Well, he'd best remember his place," Will Sanders muttered. "He may be handsome, but he's a humble player – a ruffian to most high-born folk. Lady Walden wouldn't look twice at him."

But Hugh was untroubled by Will's remark. "A cat may look at a king – or at a queen," he said. "And if she comes to the pavilion to dance, I'll be honoured to play for her."

"As will we all!" John put a hand on Hugh's shoulder. "Now, we'd best take what refreshment we can, then set ourselves to tuning the instruments. We've still a long day ahead."

The players forgot their jesting, and turned their attention to the food. Cakes and candied fruit disappeared so quickly that the platters were soon emptied. But then a shadow fell across the table, and Ben looked round.

"What's this?" Whispering Nick stood there, frowning at them. "You're paid to make music, not gorge yourselves – get to your places!"

And he watched while Lord Bonner's Men hurried back to the pavilion – where they were now to become a consort of music.

Late that afternoon, however, the smiles returned to their faces, as Hugh got his wish: Lady Imogen Walden arrived, on the arm of Sir Miles, to join in the dancing.

At that moment, the company, seated on stools, were in full musical flow with a coranto, a lively skipping dance in a three-four rhythm. The hired men who were no longer needed had been paid by John and sent home, leaving an orchestra of nine. One of the hirelings played a viol, with a second man on bass viol. There was a flute player beside Matt, who himself struggled to do his best on the hautboy. Hugh and Gabriel were skilled players of the recorder, while Solomon, with a new skin on his drum, beat a lively accompaniment. That left John and Ben on their lutes. Fortunately John was such a good lutenist that he was able to cover up the mistakes Ben made, though from the looks he gave at times he wasn't pleased. But it didn't matter too much, for the consort were in good form. A cheerful crowd had assembled, and the pavilion was filled with dancers.

When the betrothed couple entered there was applause. Sir Miles bowed to Lady Imogen, who made her curtsy. Now, as they began to dance, and Lord Bonner's players had the chance to get a proper look at her, Ben was struck by how young the lady was. In fact, she hardly looked her seventeen years. Her face was pale, the cheeks lightly coloured with vermilion, her hair dressed elegantly under a net of pearls. It appeared that Sir Miles had already lavished gifts on his bride-to-be. And despite Gabriel's doubts, Lady Imogen seemed devoted to him, smiling and hardly taking her eyes off him.

Though Ben liked watching the dancing, he forced himself to concentrate on playing his lute. Already his fingers were becoming sore again. He hoped the next tune would be one he hadn't learned, so that he could take a rest.

Outside the sun was setting, yet the festivities were only just getting into their stride. Laughter was heard above the music, and the pavilion grew hotter as it heaved with cavorting guests. Most of the young men were skilled dancers, eager to show off their steps for the ladies. On the edges of the throng, liveried servingmen stood by with jugs of wine and cordial. Through the tent's opening, Ben could see servants outside lighting torches and placing them in stands. And all the while, the music of the coranto flowed, the players plucking, blowing and beating for all their worth.

Ben was pressing hard on the frets of his lute, forming a chord of D, while with his right hand he plucked the heavy catgut strings. For a moment his gaze strayed to the dancers again – and stopped, his eyes fixing on a young serving-boy, who stood near the wall of the tent with a wine jug. His heart thumped, and his fingers ceased to work, causing John to turn with a frown.

But Ben saw only the slim figure in green and gold

livery, who was watching Sir Miles intently...and now he knew he was not mistaken. For his part, Sir Miles saw nothing but the face of his bride-to-be before him. Nor did anyone else notice when, as the couple drew nearer to him, the servant stooped to place his jug on the floor. But Ben's eyes widened as he saw the boy put a hand inside his doublet – and whip out a dagger.

For of course, it was no boy: the green eyes and the black hair tucked inside the collar had already told their tale. Ben jumped up, sending his stool flying. His lute fell to the boards with a crash, causing the orchestra to look round in alarm. But he did not hesitate. He took a flying leap from the stage, knocking people aside, causing a flurry of cries, his eyes locked upon his goal:

Mistress Jane Neale, a look of cold determination on her face as she took a step towards her enemy, Sir Miles Brandon.

Chapter Ten

As Ben had once done in Finsbury Fields, he launched himself at Jane, throwing her clean off her feet. Around him there were screams, as people scattered in all directions. But all he could think of as he hit the ground was to grab the hand with the dagger. And though she cried out in pain and anger, Jane still held on to the weapon. At once, she and Ben became locked in a fight for mastery of it.

But it did not last long. Screams gave way to shouts, and several men closed about the pair. Ben found himself hauled roughly to his feet, his arms pinned behind him. Jane was also seized, her long hair loose from the struggle. She gasped as a burly servingman wrapped his arms tightly about her – whereupon Ben cried out.

"Careful – she has a dagger! She meant to kill Sir Miles!"

There was a chorus of dismay. Luckily for Ben, however, the evidence was plain to see, as the servant gripped Jane's right hand and forced it open. There indeed was the weapon: an old, bone-handled poniard, its blade worn thin. But it had been ground to a sharp edge which glinted in the torchlight – and its purpose was crystal clear: one well-aimed thrust into Sir Miles's heart and he would have been killed.

The ladies, including Lady Imogen, had been hurried out of the pavilion. Angry men now encircled Ben and Jane. The dagger was wrenched from her hand and two servants held her arms, while another pulled off his belt to bind them. Only now was Ben aware that the music had stopped. Craning his head, he saw John trying to push his way through. Suddenly everyone was talking – only to be silenced by a voice which they all recognized: that of Sir Miles Brandon.

"The boy has saved my life!"

The man holding Ben let go of him, and stepped back. Breathing hard, his face shining with sweat,

Ben massaged his wrists, which throbbed with pain. Unsure what to do, he dropped to one knee before Sir Miles.

"Your pardon, sir," he panted. "I saw her – I mean, I saw the dagger drawn..."

"So you did," Sir Miles said. "And you acted bravely..." He gestured to Ben to stand up. But as he did so, the knight frowned. "Did you say *her*?"

Ben glanced at the prisoner, who hung her head. "Her name is Jane Neale, sir," he said. "Yet she sometimes goes as a boy."

All eyes settled upon Jane. Sir Miles gazed at her, but the girl would not look at him. Her chest heaved as she fought to catch her breath.

"Girl or boy, she's a mighty clever one," the knight said grimly. "To gain entry to my household, and pass herself off as a servant..." He broke off. Only now did the seriousness of the matter seem to dawn upon him.

There was a commotion, and at last Sir Miles's servants parted to allow John to hurry to Ben's side.

"Are you hurt?" he asked anxiously.

Ben shook his head, highly relieved that the danger had passed. But glancing at Jane again, he could not help feeling a pang of regret: she looked so forlorn and helpless. Now Sir Miles was speaking again – and at his next words, Ben was taken aback.

"Well, young master – you're the hero of the hour," the knight said, forcing a smile. "And such courage shall not go unmarked." He was recovering his wits quickly. But when a figure in black appeared, he showed his anger.

"I want to know how this assassin got in here, dressed in my livery, master steward!" he snapped. "And I will require an answer soon!"

"Indeed, Sir Miles..." Nicholas Sparrow's face was white. "No stone will be left unturned, I swear—"

He broke off, for Sir Miles had looked round sharply at Ben, as if he had only just realized what the boy player had said.

"Neale?" he echoed. "Is that her name?"

Ben nodded, and looked to John.

"That's the name she gave us, sir," John said. "I sheltered her under my roof for a few days, until she ran away..."

"Sheltered her...why was that?" Then, as if guessing this was a long story, Sir Miles held up his hand.

"No – wait. You will come to the house, John Symes, and tell me all. As will Master..." He frowned, whereupon John reminded him. "Master Button," the knight went on. "As for the girl..." He faced his steward again. "Put her under guard, until I decide what to do. Away with her!"

Finally Sir Miles looked round at his startled guests. "Good sirs – I pray you, forgive my absence for a while," he said smoothly. "Please reassure the ladies that all is well, and the small difficulty that arose is passed. Drink and make merry, for no harm is done. I'll wager the consort can manage without two of their number...Master Symes?"

John signalled to Hugh and the others, who were still on the stage. "They'll do their best, sir," he said.

There was relief all round. Men seemed eager to speak of what had happened, but were holding their tongues until their host had gone. Sparrow was marshalling the servants, ordering wine to be poured. It was over – and Ben was the saviour of the day.

Jane was being marched away – and suddenly Ben gave a start, as she raised her head to look straight at him. And her voice flew into his mind, from what seemed a long time ago: *You think you're a hero, don't you...*

But now, to his surprise, there was no malice in her eyes – only desperation. And before she disappeared from his sight, the girl silently mouthed two words: *Help me!*

His eyes widened in astonishment. After all that had happened, she was asking Ben to help her?

Once again, he thought, where Jane was concerned, nothing made sense.

Dusk was falling, and in Sir Miles's private chamber, candles had been lit. The master of Brandon Court was seated at his carved table with his future father-in-law, Lord Walden, who looked grave. Manservants stood by – and despite what had happened, their suspicious eyes fell on Ben as he and John were ushered in.

There was an uncomfortable feeling in the room, Ben thought. For one thing, to his eyes there seemed to be tension between Sir Miles and Lord Walden. But quickly, Sir Miles tried to soothe the atmosphere.

"Be seated, masters," he said, smiling at the players. "Will you take wine or ale?"

It was somewhat different to the way they were treated when they were last here. But John said they were thirsty, and would be glad of a mug of watered ale. So a servant carried stools over, while another brought cups and filled them. Then, as they sat down, Sir Miles asked John to tell him about Jane, and how she came to be a guest in his house.

The tale did not take long. Carefully leaving out the business of the stolen goblets, John told how his prentice had brought the girl home to his house in Hog Lane. She was lame and hungry, John said, and unsuited to the beggar's life she had been leading, disguised as a boy. His family took pity on her and gave her shelter – though, John added, four days later the girl was gone. But she had already told them of the hardship her family suffered. That was in the distant county of Shropshire, following the death of her father, a farmer...

Now John hesitated. Ben, too, was uneasy, for he knew that to tell Sir Miles all Jane had said would be unthinkable. But at once the knight broke in.

"Richard Neale!" he cried – and to the surprise of Lord Walden, he smacked his hand down upon the table. "I remember! He was one of my tenant farmers. A weak, sickly fellow – he died last autumn."

"A tenant?" John exclaimed. "Then the girl lied. She said the farm belonged to her family, who lost it – and the shock of being thrown off their land caused her father's death!"

He broke off, as if fearing he had said too much, but Sir Miles was nodding. "She lied to you indeed, Master Symes!" he said. "Neale died of a sickness – and as for losing the farm: his widow could not work it alone, with so many young children to look after, not to mention a frail grandmother. I gave them a cottage, at a cheap rent..." He frowned. "Did you think I would see them cast outdoors to starve? I'm a good landlord – you may ask any folk in Shropshire, as well as in the shires of Gloucester and Worcester. Besides..." The knight nodded to himself. "As I remember it, Neale's widow was married again, not long ago – yes, to a carpenter. A widower with a child of his own. They were all living together comfortably, the last I heard."

He looked puzzled. "Which leaves the question: why in heaven's name did the girl wish to kill me?"

"She...she spoke of vengeance, sir," John answered awkwardly. "Yet I think she scarcely knew what she thought – or what she was doing."

Sir Miles did not answer – and all at once, Ben had a pang of doubt. Could Sir Miles be right? Could what Jane had told them really be a pack of lies? For despite Ben's feelings for The Ironmaster, he thought Sir Miles's account rang true. The man had a lot of properties and many tenants – would he make up such a tale? Ben found himself filled with dismay at the thought that he had been taken in so readily by Jane's story.

"So..." Sir Miles was thoughtful. "The girl must be

Richard Neale's eldest child. Perhaps she was unhinged by her father's death, so that events became muddled in her mind. And she has fixed upon me, somehow, as the cause of her grief. Or perhaps she dislikes her stepfather, and has run away from home. Does that not seem a more likely tale to you?"

"It does, sir," John agreed. "Such feelings are not uncommon in folk of her age."

"True enough..." Sir Miles shifted his gaze towards Ben. "What do you say, Master Button? For it was you who brought this waif to your master. Do you now regret your action?"

Ben blinked. It seemed an odd question, and he did not know how to answer. Then all at once, another voice spoke up.

"He merely took pity on a beggar," Lord Walden said quietly. "An act of common charity... How was he to know her story was false?"

Sir Miles forced a smile. "Indeed, My Lord – you are right," he said. "And I will take a leaf from Master Button's book. If a humble player can show such charity, surely I can do the same?"

For the first time, Lord Walden turned to look at Sir Miles, whereupon the knight said, "This girl meant to take my life: that much is plain, and there are witnesses to it. By rights I should commit her to a magistrate – yet if I did she would surely hang. So I will be lenient – for she's clearly confused, or deluded. Why else would she attempt such a wicked and desperate act on someone who has shown only kindness to her family?"

Sir Miles paused – and suddenly Ben knew that whatever the man said, it had nothing to do with showing mercy to Jane. Instead, it was to make himself look wise and generous to everyone.

"No..." Sir Miles shook his head. "I'm not a vengeful man. And if the girl has fallen into madness, blaming me for her misfortunes, still I would not have her sent to the asylum of Bedlam – it's a fearful place. Instead I will hold her safely here, under lock and key, though well treated, until her stepfather can be summoned to take her home. A horse will be sent, so that he may travel swiftly. He must decide how to help the child – I'll give the man money for her keep. No doubt she's a trial to her poor family, as she has been to all of us."

There was a silence. Ben had to admit to himself that he could not think of a better outcome – whether Sir Miles was being merciful or not.

"Do I have your blessing, My Lord?" The knight raised his eyebrows at Lord Walden.

"You reason well, sir," His Lordship said. "Though

I myself feel this girl deserves punishment, I too would not see her hanged."

"Then it's agreed!" Sir Miles looked pleased with himself. "Now, but one matter remains: to thank this young player who saved me from injury – if not from death. Master Button, I'm in your debt, and be sure your patron Lord Bonner will hear of it. So, would you care to name your reward?"

Ben gulped. Beside him, he sensed John's pride in him, as well as his relief that the whole business was over. He glanced from his master to Sir Miles. "I don't know what to ask for, sir," he replied.

For now that he considered it, Ben realized he had everything he needed. He had a good home, John bought him his clothes, as well as giving him a few pence to spend...and in any case, to ask for money seemed greedy. Seeing everyone awaiting his answer, he thought hard. The only thing that came to mind was a new lute – until an idea popped into his head.

"My mother is a widow, sir," he said. "And she has not found a new husband. She's hard pressed at times, bringing up my younger brother and sister. If, er..."

He broke off. All at once he knew what his mother Mary Button would say, to hear him ask for charity. She was a proud woman, who looked after her family as well as anyone he knew.

"Don't be afraid, young fellow!" Sir Miles was smiling again. "Give her name to my steward, and I'll see that a purse is sent..." He raised his eyebrows as Ben brightened suddenly. "What now! Do you wish to change your request?"

"I do, if you please, sir," Ben answered. He explained that his mother would be uneasy at being sent money like a beggar receiving alms. However, at the cottage in Hornsey she kept chickens and a pig – though what she had always wanted, and was beyond her means, was, well—

"A cow?" Sir Miles gave a shout of laughter. "And why not, indeed? A most practical gift! I will instruct my grooms to buy the best milking cow that Smithfield can sell, and have it driven to the village of Hornsey. Does that content you?"

Ben murmured his thanks and made his bow. Inside he felt quite anxious: he hoped he had done the right thing.

"Well then..." Sir Miles looked to John. "Master Symes – I sense you're eager to return to your company. You may leave, with my thanks."

John bowed, and turned to go. Ben was about to follow – whereupon a picture came into his mind that stopped him in his tracks. And somehow, he knew what he must do. Under the gaze of every man in the room, he faced Sir Miles again.

"There is one more matter, sir..." he began, whereupon Sir Miles's smile faded.

"It may seem strange," Ben went on, "yet I would beg another favour, one that will cost nothing. It's... a matter of conscience, you might say."

He hesitated, for Lord Walden now fixed his steady gaze upon him. And it was His Lordship who spoke instead of Sir Miles.

"Make your request, Master Button," he said. And drawing a deep breath, Ben did so.

"I would like to say farewell to Jane."

Chapter Eleven

*J*ane was held in a large storeroom, which had
been hastily cleared out. There were no windows,
and the only light came from a smoky rushlight.
As they entered, Ben could see little. Then there
was a rustle of skirts, and a woman in a plain apron
got up from a stool near the doorway. The armed
man who accompanied Ben and John spoke a few
words, and at once she went out, closing the door.
Ben peered round, his eyes adjusting to the gloom –
then saw a hunched figure, sitting on the floor with
her back to the wall. Jane raised her head to look

at him, and her gaze did not waver.

The servingman spoke. "You have a few minutes, and no more," he said. "Sir Miles's orders. And I'm to remain with you the whole time."

Ben was at a loss. He had no idea how he could possibly help Jane – but he was sure that if the girl wanted to tell him something, she would not speak freely in front of the guard. Yet he guessed that nothing would persuade the man to leave them. In fact, Ben was surprised to be here at all, for when he made his request, Sir Miles was at first unwilling to grant it. He spoke of Ben putting himself in danger, and of Jane using the opportunity to try to escape. It was only when Lord Walden said that a brief farewell could do little harm, especially if Ben's master and a guard were near, that Sir Miles reluctantly gave in.

"May I sit by her?" Ben asked. "Just for a while?"

The guard hesitated, but John spoke. "She was a friend to my daughters, once," he said. "And I'll keep an eye on her."

The fellow shrugged, then nodded and sat down on the stool near the door. John remained by the wall, while, with a glance at his master, Ben crossed the room. But he had barely sat down beside Jane before she spoke urgently, her head lowered.

"Please listen," she whispered. "It's very important—"

"Sir Miles told us everything," Ben interrupted, keeping his own voice low. "Your father was a tenant – he wasn't cheated out of his farm as you said. Your mother remarried, and was given a cottage—"

"Stop!" Jane broke in. "For pity's sake, will you listen?"

Ben looked up, and saw the guard watching. But if he had heard what was said he gave no sign. John had turned away, and was squatting on his heels.

"It pains me to beg you, master hero." Jane spoke quietly, so that Ben had to lean close. "But hear me out, then judge me if you will. For if I've told lies, they're naught compared with the ones The Ironmaster tells."

Ben noticed now that the servant's livery had been taken from her. In its place, Jane wore workaday clothes that were none too clean, perhaps borrowed from a kitchen maid. He drew a breath and waited.

"Yes, Father was a yeoman farmer – a tenant," Jane said. "So was my grandfather before him. But our old landlord would never have made us leave the farm – it was everything to my family."

"Your old landlord?" Ben echoed.

"The Ironmaster bought the land off him, as he

bought up the whole valley," Jane told him. "Then he used any means he and his lawyers could find to get rid of those who lived there. I told you: so he could get the coal beneath, for his foundry."

Ben listened, realizing he was still angry with Jane for the things she had done. Yet the girl's words struck him with the same force they had done that night in the parlour, more than a week ago. He kept silent, and let her continue.

"The foundry's in the shire of Worcester," Jane went on urgently. "Once it was just a blacksmith's, before Brandon turned it into a great ironworks for the making of cannons. They're shipped down the River Severn to Bristol, and then to the English troops fighting in Ireland." She paused, somewhat breathless. "They say English guns are the best – so a man who can cast large numbers of them may make his fortune. You see now, where much of The Ironmaster's wealth comes from!"

"So his foundry makes cannons for our troops," Ben said, with a shrug. "That's why he's important… why he's in the Queen's favour—"

"That isn't all!" Jane whispered. With an anxious glance at the guard, she leaned towards Ben, wincing with pain…and only now did he notice that her hands were tied behind her back. Once again he pitied her – as he had done the first time he saw her, among a group of wretched beggars. An unpleasant thought struck him: that in a way, it was he himself who had brought her to this. She was helpless, and she needed him – but at her next words, he frowned.

"Now I'll tell you my secret," Jane said. "For whether you believe me or not, you're the only one I *can* tell."

She was breathing fast, and Ben's own pulse quickened. Part of him still suspected that the girl was not to be trusted – but the other part was eager to hear her. He knew it was his curious side: the Ben Button who could not resist a mystery. He listened, while Jane leaned as close to him as she dared.

"My father told me something, just before he died," she said. Her voice was tight, and to his surprise Ben realized that she was close to tears.

"My uncle – his brother – is a sailor, who serves on ships out of Bristol," she went on. "It was he who told Father that Brandon's cannons don't all go to Ireland. I mean, they do – but some of them go somewhere else...somewhere they shouldn't...perhaps even into the hands of England's enemies. I swear to you on my father's life, it's the truth!"

She broke off, struggling with her feelings. Ben sat very still, and waited until she whispered again.

"Father didn't know who he could trust with such tidings," she said. "For who would dare accuse a man like The Ironmaster of anything unlawful? And in any case, a few days later, Father was dead." She sighed heavily. "They say it was the sweating sickness – but he was wasting away before that. I told you: his spirit was broken when he lost the farm. So to my mind it was The Ironmaster who killed him, as surely as if he had stabbed him through the heart! My plan was to pay him back in kind – and then expose his wickedness. It's for that reason I've carried something all the way from home – something my uncle gave my father, and which my father gave to me. Now you must use it, to uncover Brandon's treachery!"

Ben stared numbly at the floor. "Treachery?" he muttered. "But how can you be sure—"

"I can't!" Jane answered. "I can prove nothing – and now I'm caught, I can only tell you what I know in my heart: that Sir Miles is one of the wickedest men in England. I told you: whatever The Ironmaster wants, he will have!"

And then Ben received the biggest shock of all. Jane shifted position, as if to ease her cramped limbs. At once there was movement across the room: the guard was alert. He watched as Jane brought her knees up to her chest – but luckily, he could not hear what followed.

"In my left shoe – behind my heel," she murmured. "Take it!" Then as Ben stiffened in alarm, she added: "It will help answer those who doubt you – for someone must reveal what Sir Miles is doing. Can't you see that?" She was desperate now. "I've no one else to turn to, Ben Button, so I must trust you! Now please take it – quickly!"

Then she drew a sharp breath, as she and Ben looked up to see the guard getting to his feet with a frown.

"That's more than enough time to say goodbye," he said. "And I've a mind to ask what all that talk was about."

Ben's mind was in turmoil, but he thought fast. "It was nothing – she was asking my forgiveness," he said.

"Forgiveness? She should ask that of my master!" the fellow snapped. "Now, I'll see you out."

Slowly Ben got up from the floor. But as he did so, he managed to half-turn towards Jane. Deftly he slipped his hand down the back of her shoe, which was too big for her – and his fingers closed on what felt like a tiny square of card. In a moment he had drawn it out, and stuffed it in his sleeve. Then, as he stood up, the girl looked into his eyes, and whispered to him for the last time.

"I've told you all," she said. "Start with the cannons, and if you can find the truth and act upon it, you will be a true hero to me – perhaps to all England!"

Then she lowered her head. Nor did she raise it again as Ben and John were ushered outside by the guard. The door was pulled shut, and a key clanked in the lock. Then there were only their footsteps as they walked away.

"Well treated – isn't that what Sir Miles said?" John looked uncomfortable as he and Ben left the house. "She may as well be in prison." He sighed. "Yet when all's said and done, she has brought it on herself. I hope it isn't long before her stepfather comes to take her home."

Ben did not answer. All he could hear were Jane's words: *the cannons go somewhere they shouldn't...Sir Miles is one of the wickedest men in England...someone must reveal what he's doing...* In his sleeve, he could feel the edges of the card. And though he knew he should tell John about it, for some reason he did not. But in any case, voices and laughter soon assailed them from all sides. They were in the torchlit gardens, crowded with Sir Miles's guests. The party rolled on, as if what happened in the pavilion were already forgotten. From there, music could be heard – Lord Bonner's Men playing manfully on, without their two lutes.

"I urge you to forget about her, Ben."

John had stopped, and was gazing at him. Ben stopped too.

"I won't ask what you talked about," his master went on. "But to my mind, that girl has a way of weaving a spell about folk, to make them believe whatever she wants. You stopped her from doing murder, and helped save her from execution – for to attempt such an act is as good as carrying it out, in the eyes of the law. We both owe her nothing. So heed my words, and put her out of your mind. Will you do that?"

Ben nodded. And though he felt that a burden had been placed upon him, with an effort he pushed the matter away. As they walked towards the great pavilion, he forced himself to concentrate on what he must do now: play his lute, until his fingers got sore all over again.

*

That night Ben slept deeply, for it was well past midnight when he crawled under the cover of his pallet. He woke in the morning to the drumming of rain on the thatch over his head – and at once the events of the day before flooded into his mind. With a start he sat up, and felt under his pillow.

He had not dared to light a candle last night, and so had not yet looked at the slip of card. Now, in the grey morning light that came through his small window, he drew it out and examined it for the first time. And his first discovery was that it wasn't a card at all.

It was a little piece of parchment, folded into squares. It cracked as Ben opened it, and its contents took him aback. He had expected a message of some kind, but instead there were only six words, which made no sense at all:

DOSCIENTAS CULEBRINAS DE HIERRO A BRETAÑA.

Whoever had written them must have struggled, for each letter was formed crudely – or perhaps hurriedly. Ben turned the parchment over, but there was nothing on the back. He turned it again, wondering why Jane had gone to so much trouble to carry it, guarding it all through her weeks of travel and hardship. Then he sat back on his pallet and frowned.

Jane had no one else to turn to – and she had entrusted the parchment to Ben. But what on earth, he wondered, did she expect him to do with it? After all, what did he know about iron founding, or cannons, or ships going from Bristol to Ireland? He knew nothing about Ireland, except that the Queen's soldiers were fighting a war there. To him it was far away – so far that it might as well be The Americas, a vast land which was as yet unexplored. How did Jane think he might go about solving what sounded like such a dark and dangerous mystery?

He sighed, and got up with a heavy heart. Yesterday he had been the hero of the hour: the boy who had saved Sir Miles's life. Today, he felt small and helpless. There was but one thing that cheered him as he got dressed: his mother would have her own cow, which he knew would delight her. Then, as he struggled into his shirt, an idea came to him.

There was one man who knew about iron founding: Ned Campion, the blacksmith. Ben could go to him when he took Brutus out – he could say he was going to see if Ned had mended the pot. Then he could enquire casually about cannons... At least it would be somewhere to start. Perhaps, after that, he could stop hiding things from John, and tell him what he had learned.

For if Ben knew anything for certain, it was that despite agreeing to John's request to forget about Jane, he could not do it. Whether she had woven a spell about him or not, his instincts told him he must puzzle away at the matter until he had uncovered something. And though it scared him, it made him burn with curiosity too.

"Cannons, young Ben? What I know about those you could write down on a playing card, and still leave room for the knave of clubs!" Ned exclaimed. But seeing his smile coming on, Ben guessed that more would follow. Trying not to look too curious, he waited.

"Cannonballs, now – that's another matter." The blacksmith sniffed, and wiped his nose with the back of a grimy hand. "I've made a few of those in my time – by royal command, you might say. Six pounders, nine pounders, even eighteen pounders. If I recall right, the biggest is a forty pounder – a mighty fearsome weapon!"

Ben was surprised to discover how much Ned knew of such things. He was wondering how he could ask him about the strange words on the scrap of parchment, which was hidden inside his doublet.

But seeing his expression, the blacksmith broke into one of his donkey laughs.

"Don't look so puzzled, boy!" he cried. "Why, 'tis simple enough work for a man of my trade. Ever since stone ones went out of use, smiths have fashioned iron cannonballs for gunners!"

"What did you mean, 'by royal command'?" Ben asked him. "Were you in the Queen's service?"

"Nay, young Ben," Ned replied. "I was prenticed to a blacksmith, and I've never done aught else."

He gazed out at the rain that still fell. Behind them, Squeaky Martin worked the bellows, while nearby sat Brutus, his leash tied to a leg of the workbench. The old hound was falling asleep from the heat of the forge.

"You hear the firing, don't ye, from the artillery yard by the Spital Field?" Ned asked, turning to Ben. "Why, 'tis near the back of your master's house!"

"Well, yes – of course I do," Ben answered, feeling somewhat foolish. Everyone knew the walled enclosure by the Hospital of St Mary Spital, behind Hog Lane. Ben was so used to the sound of gunfire he seldom gave it a thought. Soldiers practised musketry there – and sometimes fired cannons, too...

"So where d'ye think they get their shot from?" Ned asked him. "Gun-founders don't always have time to make cannonballs – too busy casting cannons. So I've made 'em to order now and then – especially at times of danger, like in the Armada year."

His face clouded at the memory. "You should have seen it, boy…all London was in a panic then, digging ditches around the city for fear we'd be invaded by Spaniards. A fat lot of good those would have done us if they had!"

Ned looked glum now, which was unlike him. "Trouble is, we may have won the day, back in fifteen-eighty-eight," he went on, "but we're still at war with Spain – and they say King Philip's building yet another Armada! Though I'll wager our good Queen Bess is keeping an eye on him – she has her spies, as she has her stout troops and seamen."

Suddenly Ned snorted. "You know something, Master Ben? In eighty-eight, our constable fled this parish, he was so scared of the Spanish. And if you ask me, old Plugg would be no better today. That man can hardly lace his own breeches!"

At that Squeaky Martin laughed so hard that he had to stop working the bellows. But instead of shouting at him, Ned broke out laughing himself. Then he stopped and gave a sigh.

"You want to know about cannons, Ben?" He scratched his grizzled head, and pointed in the direction of the city. "Well, you could always ask the gunmakers, at the foundry by Aldgate – but I wager they'll send you away. There's secrecy in their trade, and they guard it well – 'tis too important for the safety of the Queen's realm and such. They might take you for a spy – though you don't look much like one!"

Ben smiled back. Ned's idea had raised his hopes – he had not known there was a gun foundry near Aldgate. And if he was sent packing... Well, he thought he might go there anyway, and have a look for himself – even if he risked being taken for a spy. As he went out into the rain with Brutus, he was deep in thought, wondering how he might get round that danger.

It was only when he got home that he realized he had forgotten all about Alice's pot.

Chapter Twelve

When Ben left the Curtain after that afternoon's performance, he was still thinking about what Ned had told him. Though he was uneasy, he knew he could not tell John of his plans yet. He would ask permission to go into the city before supper, but instead of passing through Bishopsgate he would turn left and walk down Houndsditch to Aldgate. It should be easy to find the gun foundry – he might even hear it before he saw it.

Luckily the rain had eased off, or Lord Bonner's Men would have had a small audience. As it was, the crowd had been thin enough to set Will Sanders worrying, and as Ben and John emerged from the theatre with Solomon and Gabriel, they saw the reason. Not far off, people were clustered about a familiar red and green booth. In the distance, Higgs's mule was munching the wet grass.

"He's back!" Gabriel glared. "No wonder we had a poor house. Well this time I'll see the fellow off once and for all!"

"Better go easy, with our friend over there." Solomon pointed towards the figure of Constable Plugg, in his old feathered hat, standing at the back of the crowd. But Plugg wasn't interested in puppets, or any sort of play. Instead his eyes roamed about, looking for someone he could arrest.

Ben stood beside John. To his relief, Kate and Meg were not among the crowd. His eyes strayed to the stage of Higgs's theatre, where he could see the dragon puppet which Master Higgs had taunted them with the day he arrived. Another puppet, a knight with a little wooden sword between its fists, was fighting the dragon furiously while the crowd cheered him on.

"I know that play," Solomon said. "It's *Sir Guy of Warwick and the Dun Cow*. After Sir Guy slays the Cow of Dunsmore, he has to fight a dragon..." He

turned to Ben with a straight face. "Talking of cows...
your mother will be pleased with her gift, won't she?
Now that her son's famous, I mean – she'll likely
think you're rich as well."

Ben blushed to the roots of his hair, while the
others laughed, even Gabriel. The fact was that ever
since Ben had leaped off the stage at Brandon Court
and saved Sir Miles from a dagger thrust, he had
been the butt of the players' jokes. Solomon claimed
Ben had only done it to get out of playing his lute,
while Matt said Ben was so thirsty it was the jug
of wine he really wanted, and he had knocked
the assassin over to get it. But despite the jesting,
Ben knew the players were proud of him – including
Matt, who was eager to hear what had happened
inside Sir Miles's private chamber. The company had
talked of little else before their performance today.
And when John told them about Jane, they were
astonished at her boldness. But Ben kept to himself
what occurred later, in the storeroom, and he was
relieved when no one asked him for details.

There was a burst of applause: Higgs's show
had ended. The man himself appeared from behind
his booth, the puppet of Sir Guy still on his hand. Sir
Guy took his bow first, before the puppet master
took his. As usual, Higgs began to move round with

his hat. Then, as the crowd started to disperse, his eyes fell upon the players.

John glanced at Constable Plugg and, seeing him ambling away, turned to his fellows. "We'll speak with Master Higgs after all," he said. "But remember: I want no trouble."

So John, Ben, Solomon and Gabriel walked towards their rival, who flinched at their approach but stood his ground. With a swift movement, he emptied coins out of his hat and stuffed them inside his doublet. Then, putting the hat on, he raised his puppet.

"Well, masters..." Higgs smiled and twirled his luxurious moustache. "Did you enjoy our play?"

"They watched it for free!" the knight puppet said, in a voice of outrage. "Make 'em pay up, the skinflints!"

Master Higgs frowned. "Sir Guy – I pray you, show some charity," he said severely. "These players are likely penniless, like most of their kind – I'll not take money off poor folk!"

Gabriel bristled, but held his tongue. Solomon, however, did not. "From the princely sum you tipped out of that hat, I'd say you've taken quite a bit of money off poor folk, friend," he said. "Perhaps you should buy us players a supper!"

Higgs kept his smile. "Your pardon, but I have

other plans," he said – then blinked as John raised his hand.

"What a splendid idea!" John exclaimed. "But I'll buy the supper, Master Sol. I think after yesterday's hard work our company deserves a treat. The White Hart's my choice, by Bishopsgate." He looked at the others, who gazed at him in surprise, then faced the puppet man again.

"I mean it, Master Higgs," he said. "You will be my honoured guest, and after we've dined we'll talk business. If we couldn't reach agreement before, let's try again on a full stomach, shall we? No tricks, and no false dealing – you have my word. Now, what do you say?"

There was silence. Higgs appeared as surprised as the players. Finally, he managed a nod. Ben was so taken aback, he had almost forgotten his idea of going to the gun foundry. But in any case, his plans were thrown into disarray by John's next words.

"Then that's settled!" he said, smiling. "Ben, off to the theatre with you and tell the others – all are invited. If anyone's already gone, ask Will to send a message: supper in an hour, at the White Hart! Hurry!"

So Ben could do nothing but run back to the Curtain. He was torn between the prospect of a lively meal with his fellows – with Harry Higgs as the surprise guest – and the knowledge that his spying trip would have to wait.

In a private room at the White Hart Inn, the table was spread with the best meal that John's purse would allow.

There was a roast goose, and a platter of snipe. There was also woodcock with a huge dish of cabbage and onions, and a bowl of spring sallet to keep it company. For dessert there was cheese with sugar and sage, all of it washed down with the landlord's best ale. It may not have been as good as the fare Lord Bonner's Men had got at Brandon Court, but to them it was still a feast. And of course, John's real reason for the supper had little to do with feasting – and a lot to do with reaching agreement with Harry Higgs.

The puppet master, for his part, soon got over his unease at being seated among his rivals – even though Will and Gabriel glared at him to begin with. But as the evening turned into night, and candles were lit against the dark, the glaring ceased. For the players liked nothing better than celebration, and the chance to swap tales and jokes. At last even Will, rosy-cheeked with drink, was slapping Higgs on the back and telling him to forget about that bump on the head, for it was naught; while Gabriel began talking of moustaches, on which he was a noted expert, and grudgingly admitted that the puppet master's was one of the finest he had seen. Solomon, meanwhile, was asking Higgs which got the more laughs: *Gawain and the Green Knight,* or *Sir Guy of Warwick and the Dun Cow?*

The room was warm, and loud with chatter and laughter. Someone called for a song, and soon voices rose in harmony on old favourites like *Three Ravens* and *Oh Mistress Mine*. And it was during the chorus of *Three Ravens* that Matt Fields moved to Ben's side of the table, and pulled up a stool next to him.

"Well, Master B," he said quietly. "It's time you told me all about your sharp-tongued friend, Mistress Neale. From what John said today, it was her I saw with Kate and Meg at the puppet show, wasn't it? And it seems she's the same person, disguised as a beggar, that I helped to escape from Plugg with my splendid fit! So I think I've a right to know what you've been keeping to yourself, wouldn't you say?"

Ben's mouth was full of cheese, and he took his time eating it. His first instinct was to say little. But seeing Matt's eyes upon him, he began to have second thoughts. Perhaps he could confide in someone after all – for the things Jane had told him weighed heavily on his mind. In fact, he realized, he would be glad of any help he could get. So finally he swallowed the cheese, took a drink and set down his mug.

"Very well," he said. "But swear first that you'll speak not a word of what I tell you."

"It sounds important," Matt said. "If you wish it – I swear."

So while the song soared about them, Ben leaned close to Matt and told him all about Jane: from the morning he and Brutus caught her robbing a house, to the talk he had with her in the storeroom at Brandon Court when she told him her secret. Yet without really knowing why, he did not mention the square of parchment with the strange words on it. Then he sat back while his fellow player took in the news. And now even Matt, who was seldom surprised by anything, was dumbstruck.

"Well, you're in a quandary, aren't you?" he said at last. "What will you do?"

"I'm not sure yet," Ben answered. But he felt relieved to have told someone. Seeing Matt's frown deepening, he added: "I asked Ned the blacksmith about cannons. He told me of the gunmakers by Aldgate, but he said they'd send me away..."

"The foundry! What do you expect to find there?" Matt asked.

Ben shrugged. "It's somewhere to start, isn't it?"

At that, a smile spread over Matt's freckled features. "You mean you've hatched one of your *plans*?" He shook his head. "You can't resist poking about, can you? I never knew anyone who's so drawn to a mystery – like a wasp to a jam pot."

"But what if it's true about the cannons?" Ben asked, keeping his voice low. "I mean, would you trust a man like Sir Miles Brandon?"

"Would you trust this girl – a runaway and a thief?" Matt countered.

Ben hesitated. Into his mind came a picture of Jane, sitting against the wall with her hands tied. She had entrusted him with the parchment – and for better or worse, he must trust her too.

"Yes – I believe I would," he said at last.

It was Matt's turn to hesitate. "Well – then you'd better count me in," he said. "Perhaps I could do with a bit of an adventure, too."

Ben's heart lifted. He and Matt had made a good team before – and already, he was thinking fast.

"Tomorrow's Sunday," he said, "and there will be no one at the foundry. But suppose we had a reason to call there on Monday morning?"

"You mean, in disguise?" Matt's face fell. "Look – if you're thinking of playing my mother again, I refuse to come!"

"I wasn't," Ben said, and picked up his mug. "Let me think of something else."

Both boys looked round then, for the song had finished, and John was on his feet calling for attention. "My friends, I have tidings to announce!" He wore his broadest grin, which meant good news. "Our guest, Harry Higgs, master of puppets, and I have reached agreement. For a small fee, he will move his theatre across London tomorrow, to trouble – I mean, to entertain – folk on the South Bank, by the Rose and Swan theatres. I've said he's welcome to join us at St Leonard's on the day of the Whitsun Ale. After that he proposes to go travelling again, into...well, into other parts."

John broke off, for there was a sigh of relief from all sides of the table. Turning to the puppet master, John raised his mug and asked the players to join him in a toast to seal the bargain. So, as one, they got to their feet and drained their cups, before cheering Harry Higgs to the rafters.

Graciously the fellow rose and made his bow, twirling his huge moustache.

*

Sunday was a blustery day, and having little to do in the afternoon, Ben went for a walk to think about the morrow. He was crossing the Fields when he saw Tom the rat-catcher coming towards him. Peascod trotted beside him on a leash.

"There's no peace for me even on the Sabbath, Master Ben," Tom said, with a grin. His pole was across his shoulder as usual, with two dead rats dangling from it. "Now I'm called to Brandon Court – can you believe that? The grandest house, owned by the richest man hereabouts...'tis rare that I'm so honoured! I've even changed my attire, see?"

Ben looked, and saw the same baggy breeches Tom always wore. But the patched shirt had been replaced by a cleaner one, with a scrap of old lace about the neck.

"It looks very fine, Master Tom." Ben was wondering whether the rat-catcher knew what had happened at Sir Miles's betrothal party – for Tom was as eager for gossip as Ned Campion. But in a moment, the question was answered.

"I've been in the city," Tom said. "Got back this morning... Did you and your fellows perform for Sir Miles, like I heard you would?"

Ben didn't want to speak of his adventure: Tom would only ply him with questions. "We did – and

now you say they've called you to Brandon Court?"
he said, to change the subject. "What is it – rats,
moles or...?"

"Rats!" Tom gave a chuckle. "I hope the little
varlets kept out of sight while all those lords and
ladies strutted about – that would have spoiled their
party, wouldn't it?"

Ben nodded, and bent down to stroke Peascod. As
he did so, Tom raised a hand to shield his eyes.

"Here now," he muttered. "Who's this?"

Ben straightened, realizing he could hear hooves.
He looked round to see a horseman in dark clothes
trotting towards them along the lane from Moorgate.
Seeing Ben and Tom, the man slowed his mount, then
drew rein a short distance away. He looked down at
them, then raised a gloved hand sharply.

"I seek a big house, with a fountain. Do you
know it?"

Beside him, Ben felt Tom tense. But he was taken
aback himself; for though there were folk of many
nations in London, this man's voice was strange to
him. He had never heard an accent like it. He looked
up to meet the rider's eyes – and felt himself go cold
from head to foot.

It wasn't the flinty gaze, or the cruel mouth; it
wasn't the heavy black beard, nor even the livid scar

that ran down the fellow's cheek – though perhaps it was all those things together...

Peascod growled and went into a crouch, causing Tom to speak sharply to him. But all Ben could do was lower his eyes.

For he had stared into the face of a man without feelings: the face of a hardened villain.

Chapter Thirteen

*B*en and Tom Slyte watched the mysterious horseman ride away, urging his horse to a canter. Tom wore a grim expression, while Ben was still uneasy. He knew that Tom could have told the man he was going to Brandon Court himself, and would walk with him. Instead, he had pointed the way, and waited for the fellow to ride off.

"Well, you can knock me down flat!" Tom said. "I haven't heard that manner of speech in ten years – not since I signed up as a soldier in the Low Countries."

Seeing Ben's look of surprise, he shrugged. "'Tis

not something I like to speak of. Tales of blood and thunder, smoke and cannon – they're not for Tom Slyte. The day I got back to England in one piece, I swore I'd put those sights behind me and forget 'em." Tom frowned. "But it's not easy...especially when a fellow springs up out of nowhere and talks like a Spaniard!"

"A Spaniard?" Ben was astonished. "But we're at war with Spain, aren't we?"

"That we are," Tom replied, tugging at his beard. "And now I think on it, I've a better notion: I believe he's a Portugee. Their country's next door to Spain, you might say – Portugal, that is. It's under Spanish rule, but a few Portugee folk come here from time to time. They talk similar to your Spaniard. But when you've heard the tongue like I have, you can tell the difference."

Ben had had no idea that Tom had once been a soldier. He wondered if there were other men he knew who could tell similar tales. To Ben and his friends, war was something that happened in distant places. Now, along with Ned Campion's talk of Armadas, it did not seem quite so far away.

"Well – no use dwelling on it." Tom cleared his throat and spat. "I can't stay, Master Ben. There's work waiting..." He frowned. "I hope I don't run into that fellow at Brandon Court – he's a bad lot, if I'm any judge. What would a man like that be wanting with Sir Miles, d'ye think?"

Ben did not know. He watched Tom move off, with the rats bobbing on his pole and Peascod tugging at the leash. Then he walked homeward, deep in thought.

The next morning he and Matt arrived outside the gun foundry, at the far end of Houndsditch, by Aldgate.

From the street it looked like an ordinary house. But from behind came a great din of banging, clanging and scraping, the sounds of a busy workshop. The two boys wheeled the wooden barrow they had brought up to the door, and knocked loudly.

The barrow was Matt's idea. Ben had come to his house an hour ago, thinking that they could pose as prentices from one of the founders in Lothbury, in the city. They would ask for scrap metal for their master to fashion into bowls and basins. Matt knew a neighbour with a barrow, and managed to borrow it. Then, garbed in workaday clothes and whistling cheerfully, the two had rattled their way from Matt's house in Thames Street, up Fish Street Hill, along

Fenchurch Street and out through the big stone gatehouse at Aldgate.

Ben had only a vague plan, for he was not sure what he was looking for. He had lain awake since dawn – but it seemed the more he pondered Jane's secret, and the more he stared at the parchment, the less he understood. However, he had managed to memorize the words: *DOSCIENTAS CULEBRINAS DE HIERRO A BRETAÑA* – though he hadn't a clue what they meant. He had told Matt to let him do the talking, and to trust to luck.

He was jolted out of his thoughts by the clatter of a bolt. The door swung inwards, and a man in a leather apron appeared, scowling.

"What do you want?"

Ben touched his forehead. "If it please you, sir, can ye spare any old scrap? Shavings, or aught ye don't need, for our master…"

"Shavings?" The man echoed. "You mean scurf, don't ye?" He gave a snort. "What they teach you lads today I can't fathom!" But the fellow called over his shoulder.

"Master Moore! Prentices wanting scurf! Shall I let 'em in?"

Peering inside the doorway, Ben saw a passage that led through the building to a yard behind. There was a shout from somewhere, and the man faced them again. "Come on, then," he said, moving off. "But mind you keep out of the way!"

Concealing their excitement, Ben and Matt heaved the barrow up a step and trundled it along the echoing passage to the yard – then stopped. They had almost collided with several men in blackened aprons, wheeling a heavy cannon out of a wide doorway. Puffing and heaving, they manoeuvred the gun near to a wall, where a prentice slid wedges under the wheels. Then, with a glance at the newcomers, all of them went back inside the workshop.

"Scurf, ye wanted?"

Ben and Matt looked round to see an old man, bald save for a fringe of white hair. They guessed that he was Master Moore, though if he were in charge he looked no different to the other foundry men. Like them, he wore a dirty apron, and his shirtsleeves were rolled up to show thick, sunburned arms.

"If you please, sir," Ben replied. "My master's a thrifty man, and metals are so costly..."

"What's your master's name?" the old man asked. His tone was suspicious.

"It's, er..." Ben searched for a name, furious with himself for not having one ready. But Matt came to his rescue.

"Jones, sir," he answered. "Newly come to London from...from Norwich. He was a journeyman there, and is setting up his own shop in Lothbury—"

"I thought so!" Master Moore snorted. "No London founder would send boys here – this is the royal foundry, where ordnance is made for the Tower! 'Tis not open house, for prentices to wander in. Your master should learn better!"

Matt glanced at Ben. The trip looked doomed, almost before it had started. Frantically Ben tried to think of something – then a bold idea came to him: why not try telling the truth?

"Forgive me, sir," he said. "But we were not plain with you. There's no Master Jones, and we're not prenticed to any founder. We're players, from the theatre."

Beside him, he heard Matt groan under his breath. But both stood and waited, while the founder gazed at them in surprise.

"Players! Then what in heaven's name are you doing here?"

"We...we need your help," Ben answered, his mind working fast. "I'm ordered to find out about cannons, in time for our next play – or I'll get a beating. My fellow and I –" he indicated Matt, who struggled to keep a straight face – "we're to act

gunners on a ship, you see, and we don't know how."
He put on a grin. "We've neither of us seen a gun,
close-up."

There was a moment's silence. Then Master Moore
turned his face to the sky, and gave a great bellow
of laughter.

"Well, I never heard the like!" he cried. "Roll me
up and stuff me down a gun barrel, for I'm limp
as wadding!" He wiped his eyes, shoulders heaving.
Then he shook his bald head, and gazed at them
both.

"Not seen one close-up, you say? Well, I don't
suppose it would do any harm..." He gestured to the
cannon by the wall. "You may look at that one, and
I'll tell you what I can," he said. "It's not made for
a ship, but they're all of a kind... Will that save you
from a beating?"

Ben nodded, while Matt sighed with relief. The
two of them followed Master Moore over to the
cannon. Soon they were listening attentively while
the old man talked.

It was an army culverin, which fired a ball of
eighteen pounds. Its iron barrel was six feet long, with
great hoops about it. It was mounted on a wooden
carriage, with wheels thicker than a cartwheel.
Master Moore ran a hand over the gun as he described

it, clearly taking a pride in his craft. Ben had to admire the skill that had gone into making it – though what mayhem a culverin might cause on a battlefield, he did not like to think upon.

"Navy guns, now..." Master Moore fingered his white beard. "I can't speak of those. Indeed, I would commit treason if I told you what cannon the Queen's vessels carry. Though any sailor will tell you they sit on truck carriages, and poke through ports in the ship's side. But think of this one, and you won't go far wrong."

He fell silent, and Ben realized that the lesson was over. But something Master Moore had said struck him – and suddenly he knew what it was: *culverin*. The word sounded oddly like one of those on the parchment...it was here in his doublet, but Ben did not dare take it out. Instead he asked casually: "You wouldn't know what *culebrinas* means, would you, master?" Then at once he regretted it – for Master Moore's face darkened.

"What do you mean?" he demanded.

"I...well, I heard it somewhere, I think," Ben answered. "It sounded like—"

"I know what it sounded like," the gunmaker broke in. "Don't you try and play games with me, boy!" He took a step closer, so that Ben flinched.

Beside him, he sensed Matt was preparing to run.

"You said *culebrinas*," Master Moore went on. "That's not an English word, is it? It's Spanish – and it's an insult, for it means 'snakes'! So what exactly are you trying to say to me, boy? Eh?"

Ben gulped – but it was Matt who saved the day. "Forgive him, master," he blurted out. "He's always picking up useless bits of knowledge like that. 'Buttonhead', I used to call him – I should call him 'Clutterhead' instead!"

There was a tense moment before, to the relief of both boys, Master Moore calmed down – though he still looked suspiciously at Ben. "Well, he's a curious young fellow, all right," he said. "Are all you player folk so nosy?"

"This one is," Matt said, jerking a thumb at Ben. "No idea how to behave. If you ask me, he deserves a beating to teach him some manners."

It was clear now that they were overstaying their welcome, so quickly Ben thanked Master Moore and said they would be on their way. Although at the time he had not taken them to heart, he now recalled Ned Campion's words – and realized that if he'd kept on asking questions, he might have been taken for a spy after all!

He followed Matt towards the doorway. But they

had barely gone six paces before the old man called out. Both boys froze.

"Aren't you forgetting something?"

They turned – and saw Master Moore pointing to the barrow. Ben went to take the handles, and Matt came up beside him.

"That's the last time I go on one of your poking-about missions," he muttered. "And I don't want to hear any more about cannons. I've a mind to give you a smacking myself!"

That night Ben lay on his pallet, unable to sleep. The more he turned things over in his mind, the more muddled they got. After all the trouble he had gone to, all he had really learned from his visit to the gun foundry was that the words on the parchment were Spanish, and one meant "snakes". So what on earth could the message be about? And how could he ever understand it?

Once again, he thought about Jane. And in spite of himself, he began to wonder if her suspicions against Sir Miles Brandon were figments of her imagination. After the company's performance that afternoon, Ben had sat in the tiring room and listened to the players' gossip. Gabriel Tucker had spoken with one of Sir Miles's gardeners, a man he knew, and learned how Jane had managed to get into Brandon Court.

"It seems she climbed over the wall by night," the little player said. "She stole a set of clothes, and hid until morning. Then she mixed with the extra servants Whispering Nick had hired, and started carrying things about, bold as brass! And no one even noticed her!"

"Except our boy player," Hugh said, with a smile at Ben. "If you ask me, the girl has as much reason to thank him as Sir Miles. For he saved her from death, too."

But lying in the dark now, Ben took no comfort from Hugh's words. Jane had said he must try to put a stop to what she called Sir Miles's "treachery". But even if her accusations were true, how was he to do such a thing?

Eventually he drifted off into a troubled sleep, and dreamed that he was on a ship at sea, with cannons firing and men shouting. Matt was there, calling to him, but Ben couldn't hear what he said. He grew desperate, knowing it was important. There were other noises too: a banging and rattling. The noise got louder – and suddenly Ben was wide awake, realizing it was not part of his dream at all. He sat up, hearing a continued tapping – and in an instant he was out of bed, hurrying across the cold boards in his bare feet, and throwing open the small window.

A figure rose up, and Ben would have started had he not recognized the man's smell before he saw the face: Tom Slyte, out of breath, was lying flat on the sloping thatched roof, holding on tightly with one hand. With the other he had been knocking on the window. As it opened, he breathed a sigh.

"Praise be to heaven!" he panted. "I'm no polecat, Master Ben – if I slide off here I'll break my neck! Forgive the hour, but can I come in? I've a message that's private, and I've sworn to deliver it in secret."

Ben went to his stool, threw the clothes off it and carried it to the window. Grunting and heaving, Tom squeezed himself through the gap and got down. Then he sat on the stool, getting his breath back.

"A message?" Ben could not contain his curiosity. "From who?"

"She said she's a friend of yours," Tom answered, breathing heavily. "And it was a matter of great importance. She goes by the name of—"

But at once Ben knew, and finished the sentence himself.

"Jane Neale!"

Chapter Fourteen

The two of them sat and talked in the near darkness, Ben on the floor and Tom on the stool. Or rather Ben listened, while Tom talked.

"I couldn't risk Brutus hearing," he said. "He'd have woken up half the street. So I found a barrel to stand on, and shinned up the wall. I promised the girl I'd speak to you and no one else."

Ben nodded, controlling his impatience. He knew Tom would take his time with a tale.

"Well now..." The rat-catcher rubbed his beard. "You know I like to catch up with the news. And when the kitchen folk at Brandon Court gave me a bit of supper on Sunday, I heard about what you did..." He peered at Ben. "You're a close one, aren't you – saving Sir Miles's life? But maybe you didn't want to boast of it?"

Sensing Ben's unease, Tom let the matter drop. "Anyway, I also heard how you went to see that girl," he went on. "And today, when I went back to Brandon Court – for there's rats enough there for a week's work – well, this afternoon, knock me flat if I didn't see her myself!"

"You saw Jane yourself?" Ben exclaimed. "Where?"

"In the gardens," Tom answered. "She was taking the air, with a fellow guarding her. From all the gossip, I knew right away who she was. It turns out Sir Miles has gone away, and old Whispering Nick with him, so things are a bit slack. Else they'd never have let her outside again after what happened, would they?"

Ben could hardly bear to wait. "So, you spoke with Jane...?"

"She spoke with me, more like," Tom told him. "I confess I was curious to see the girl who pulled a dagger on Sir Miles. So I walked by her with Peascod, and slowed down so she could pat him. She said she was a farm girl, who had dogs herself once. Then, when the guard wandered off a little way, she asks if

I knew a Ben Button, in Hog Lane! When I said I did, she begged me to come here."

They were getting to the important part. And at Tom's next words, Ben felt a chill down his spine.

"It touches on that evil-looking cove." Tom lowered his voice as if the walls might hear. "The one with the scar, who we saw in the Fields." He hesitated. "Seems the girl saw him at Brandon Court. And when she asked me if I'd seen him too, I told her I thought he was a Portugee – well, then she gets excited. Now..." Tom scratched his head, and looked uneasy. "Here's the nub of it, Master Ben. I don't like it, but I'm a soft-hearted fool, so when Mistress Jane begged me to tell you, I said I would. I confess I took to the girl – for she's a brave little thing, when all's said and done. And it looks to me as if Sir Miles's servants have a soft spot for her already."

Tense as a bow, Ben waited – and heard the words that he knew at once would put him in real danger.

"She says you must go to Brandon Court tonight, soon as you can," Tom told him. "And wait near the fountain. You'll hear something that'll help you, she says."

The rat-catcher fell silent as Ben took in the news, then with a sigh, he got to his feet. "Now I'd best be gone, the way I came in," Tom said. "I only hope the thatch holds." He put his hand on the window frame, and turned back to Ben.

"I've delivered the message like I promised," he said. "But in truth, Master Ben, I wouldn't go sneaking into Brandon Court – nor would I tangle with a man like Sir Miles. What you do is your business – but be careful now, you hear me?"

Then, as an afterthought, he added: "And I was never here – nor do I know Mistress Jane. You understand me?"

Ben managed a nod – then suddenly, he remembered the parchment. And at once he knew that here was an opportunity not to be missed, for if Tom recognized the Spanish tongue, perhaps he understood a little of it too. He hesitated, but only for a second: once again he needed to trust someone, as he had trusted Matt.

"Master Tom – I'm truly grateful to you for coming," he said. "But it could be you can help me further."

Tom raised his brows. "How might I do that?"

"There are some words…I think they're Spanish," Ben said. "I…I overheard them, but I don't know what they mean. Perhaps you would know?"

Tom shrugged. "I might," he said.

So as clearly as he could, Ben spoke aloud the words from the parchment, as well as he could remember them:

"Doscientas culebrinas de hierro a Bretaña."

Slowly, Tom let go of the window frame. "Where in heaven's name did you hear that?" he muttered. Then, seeing Ben's unwillingness to answer, he frowned. "Well now – if you'd said only *'Doscientas culebrinas'*, I'd have been mighty puzzled," he went on. "For *'doscientas'* means 'two hundred', and *'culebrinas'* means 'snakes'. Two hundred snakes!"

But it was Tom's next words that took Ben's breath away. "But when you put 'em with *'hierro'*," he went on, "that puts a whole new meaning on it. For *'hierro'* means 'iron' – and 'iron snake' is a Spanish name for a kind of cannon. So all together, Master Ben, it means two hundred cannons."

He shrugged. "As for the last bit – well, to my mind, *'Bretaña'* sounds like Spanish for Britain. So I suppose it means 'two hundred cannons to Britain'. Does that make any sense to you?"

Ben did not answer. The words may not have made sense, but he felt sure of one thing now: the parchment Jane had carried with her all the way across England was very important after all. *Two hundred cannons*, it said – in Spanish.

In the storeroom Jane had voiced her fears that the cannons from Sir Miles's foundry might be going to England's enemies – and England's greatest enemy was Spain. But the message said *Two hundred cannons to Britain* – so what could it mean?

He looked up, to see Tom eyeing him. "I hope that's some help to you, Master Ben," he said. "Now, if you wouldn't mind giving *me* a helping hand...?"

Quickly Ben helped Tom climb out, thanking him again for his pains. His mind was in a whirl, but he waited until he had seen the rat-catcher clamber safely down to the street. Then he went back to his pallet and sat down heavily. Tom's special odour still lingered in the attic: a smell of rats and moles, mixed with the scent of lavender and rue.

For some minutes Ben sat there, thinking hard about what Tom had told him, and forced himself to face something he didn't like one bit: that despite the danger he might face, he must do Jane's bidding, and go to Brandon Court. In fact he should go soon, for if he thought about it too long he would never do it – something he would likely regret. Yet the idea scared him from head to foot.

The casement was still open, for he had not closed it after Tom went. And that was the way Ben should go too, or he would wake Brutus. In the dark, he dressed hurriedly, hoping that Kate and Meg wouldn't hear from their chamber below...although it seemed they had not heard Tom. Nervously Ben got onto the stool, grasped the window frame and heaved himself up. Soon he was through, with the chilly night air about him. Then he half-clambered, half-slid down the steep thatched roof. For a moment he dangled precariously above the ground, gripping the thatch – then, looking below, he saw that the barrel Tom had spoken of was still there, just visible in the gloom. Carefully Ben lowered himself onto it – then he was down, with the solid earth of Hog Lane beneath his feet.

He stood listening, but there was no sound from within the house. So without further delay he hurried round the corner into Bishopsgate Street, which was quiet, and ran swiftly along it to the entrance to Finsbury Fields. Then he was trotting through the grass, and the darkness swallowed him.

This time Ben had no blazing torch to light his way: only the pale light of a three-quarter moon. He stumbled over hillocks and slipped into soggy ditches, and in no time his clothes were wet and muddy. But he knew the direction of Brandon Court, and tried to keep to the same course he and John had followed that first night. To his relief, after a while he saw a familiar point of light: the torches on the gateposts. Minutes later he was approaching the gates – and here he came up against his first real obstacle: the entrance to the wooden bridge was closed off, by a barrier with spikes on top. Grimly, Ben realized there was nothing for it: he would have to swim the moat.

Ben was as good a swimmer as any boy from his village who had splashed across Hornsey pond on a hot summer's day. Yet he hesitated, for he had no idea how deep the water was. Then all at once, he felt ashamed: had not Jane braved both moat and wall to get herself inside Brandon Court? And if she could do it, surely Ben Button could too.

Moving away from the bridge, where the water glittered with reflected torchlight, he followed the moat as it bent round a corner. Then he stopped where the wall faced west. Behind here, if he remembered correctly, were only lawns and flower beds. So he pulled off his shoes and, taking a few deep breaths, slid down the bank into the cold water – only to find himself standing on a stony bed. The moat was barely three feet deep, and came just above his waist.

For of course, it wasn't a real moat: it was a sham, built by Sir Miles for the purpose of showing off. Ben could have laughed at his own fears. He waded across, put his shoes on and was soon gazing up at the wall, seeking a place to climb.

This proved more difficult. The walls of Brandon

Court were built of solid London brick, with no footholds that Ben could see. Nor was there a tree or bush to aid him. For a while he walked along the narrow bank between wall and moat, taking care not to slip. Finally, as he was beginning to think the climb was impossible, he stopped: something was floating in the water below him. Squinting in the poor light, he saw what looked like a log. So with hopes rising he slid down, stepped into the moat again and found what turned out to be an oak beam. At once Ben seized it and dragged it up the bank. Then it was a simple task to lean it against the brickwork, to form a rather slippery ladder. Gripping the wet beam with both hands, and shivering a little, Ben worked his way upwards until he could poke his head above the wall...then he gasped, and ducked down at once.

No more than ten yards away was Sir Miles's famous fountain, clearly visible in the moonlight – and there was someone crouching beside it!

Heart pounding, Ben kept low, clinging to the beam and trying not to lose his grip. In the silence he chided himself for his carelessness – he knew that Sir Miles had guards about, day and night. If Ben had been seen, he was in real trouble. Finally, summoning all his nerve, he raised his head very slowly – then froze: the figure had gone!

He listened, but heard nothing save the call of a night bird. There was no movement anywhere, and he began to wonder if he had imagined seeing someone. Across the grounds, the huge shape of Sir Miles's house filled the night sky. There were lights at some of the windows, but all seemed quiet.

Ben gazed uneasily over the moonlit gardens. He saw the place where the great pavilion had stood, in which he had saved Sir Miles from Jane's attack. Now there was only grass, with a gardener's wheelbarrow lying on it. He scanned the lawns and beds, the paths with their marble statues, but saw no one. Though he was afraid, he knew he must not linger – he was too exposed where he was. So, throwing a leg across the wall, which was capped with smooth stone, he scrambled over and dropped eight or nine feet onto soft earth. Then, half-crouching, he hurried across the flower bed and along a path towards the fountain.

The fountain was a statue, fashioned into the shape of some mythical beast with a long tail. It stood in the middle of a walled pool, but of course it was silent now, with no gardener's boy to pump the water. Quickly, Ben began to search for anything that might look out of place. But very soon, as he looked around the stone edge of the pool, then at the paths and flower beds, a sense of hopelessness came upon him.

He must come to the fountain, Jane had said – so shouldn't there be a message of some kind? But if so, where was it? In a pouch or a pot, or buried somewhere? Could it even be under the water?

With growing despair, Ben peered into the dark pool, but could see nothing. So he began sifting through the nearby flower beds. His hands were soon sticky with soil, yet still he dug, working his way along. Then he stopped, and sat down heavily on the ground.

It was futile, if not plain foolish. He could search like this all night. Now anger swept over him – and at once he found himself blaming Jane. It was she who had brought him to this, of course: taking risks, not to mention sneaking out by night – something he'd never done in all the time he had lived in John's house. Once again it seemed Jane had let him down. In fact, when had she brought him anything but trouble?

With a heavy heart, Ben realized there was no message – and nothing to do but get away, as quickly as possible. Wiping his hands on his breeches, he got to his feet. He was about to make his way back to the wall, when...

"Ben Button?"

It was little more than a whisper, but the voice was so close Ben nearly jumped out of his skin. Whirling round, he saw a figure standing just a few feet away – the same one he had seen, he guessed, only minutes ago.

"I had to wait, until I was sure you hadn't been spotted." The boy who spoke was taller than Ben, dressed in plain workaday clothes and a cap. Now he beckoned urgently.

"Come with me – hurry now."

He turned and strode away, across a flower bed towards the wall, where he disappeared. Heart still thudding, Ben followed. Soon he was in shadow, and it was too dark to see the other's features clearly.

"This comes from Mistress Jane," the boy said. "But then you know that by the rat-catcher, don't ye?"

He was a servant, somewhat harsh of speech. Ben was about to make reply, but the other cut him off sharply.

"I've little time," he said. "I was going to take you to a window, where she could speak to you herself. I can't now though, for they've moved her back to that storeroom, and there's a guard. But I've remembered her words, so you'd best do the same. Ready?"

"Ready," Ben said.

The boy drew a deep breath. "She says the man with the scar who was here is known to her from

Coalbrookdale. He's named Perez, and he works for Sir Miles. Mistress Jane had been put to work in the gardens here, weeding and such. And yesterday she saw that fellow Perez walking there, talking with Sir Miles. So Jane moved closer, trying to hear what they said, before a gardener stopped her. Then Sir Miles caught sight of her and went wild – told the guard to take her back in the house. Soon after that Sir Miles ordered fast horses, and took off with Perez at full gallop. Master Sparrow's gone too."

The boy paused for breath. Then, with Ben hanging on every word, he went on: "Now – this is what's most important, Mistress Jane says. For she heard a little of what they said to each other before she was spotted. Perez said that the goods weren't going out quick enough – they must be speeded up, he said, or their customer would be angry. And that's why Sir Miles has gone off in a hurry to his foundry. Jane says you should know by now what the goods are. So you must act fast, she says – for who else will?"

Ben stared into the dark, at the face of the boy he could barely see. His heart was racing.

"That's all," the other said shortly. "Now I'm away – for if I'm caught..." He broke off. "It seems Mistress Jane trusts you," he went on. "I didn't think you'd come, but I was wrong about that. Now you'd best get yourself out, before someone sees you. The guard by the gate won't sleep for ever – and when he wakes, he'll be bringing the dogs round!"

His thoughts in a whirl, Ben nodded and turned to go – then froze. How was he to get back up the wall?

But the answer to that came swiftly. "Here's your foothold," the servant said, and nudged Ben. Feeling downwards, he found that the lad had put his hands together to make a step. Ben was about to place his foot on it...then he hesitated.

"Why do you wait?" the other demanded. "Move!"

"You've shown a great deal of courage," Ben began – but once more, the voice came out of the darkness.

"There's naught I wouldn't chance to help Mistress Jane," the boy snapped. "And whatever you might think of Sir Miles's servants, we're not all like him! Now climb up, before I leave you here!"

So Ben stepped onto the clasped hands – and was immediately lifted skywards, with a strength that surprised him. Clumsily, he grasped the top of the wall and pulled himself up. Then, without looking back, he shinned over and dropped down the other side. Within seconds he was wading the moat, scrambling up the far bank, and plunging into the dark.

But even as he ran from Brandon Court, he heard the distant bark of a dog. Whoever the young servant was, Ben thought grimly, he had indeed risked everything to help Jane.

He could only hope that the boy had got out of the way in time.

Chapter Fifteen

The next morning, Ben knew that John would be angry. In fact, he expected him to be angrier than he had ever been since the day Ben had come to live with him.

They were in the front chamber, with rain dripping outside the window. The downpour had started in the night, some time after Ben managed to climb back up the thatch and crawl through his window into the attic. He had been breathless and sweaty from running, his clothes dirty, his shoes and hose soaked. He was so tired after his adventure that he had fallen asleep at once – to be woken with a start, in full daylight, by Alice calling to him to stir himself. When he appeared, stumbling bleary-eyed down the stairs in his spare set of clothes, he looked the picture of guilt. But when he said he had something of great importance to tell, John steered him into the small room and sat him down. Then and there, under the gaze of his master, Ben at last unburdened himself of the whole affair. For he knew now that it was too important to keep to himself.

He began with what Jane had told him in the storeroom at Brandon Court. He spoke of the parchment and, drawing it sheepishly out of his sleeve, handed it to John, who took it in silence. Then he told of his visit to the gun foundry, and what he had learned from Master Moore, from Ned Campion, and from Tom Slyte, about cannons. He also mentioned the sinister horseman he and Tom had met with in Finsbury Fields. He had already decided not to speak of Tom's night-time visit, let alone his own foray to Brandon Court, for he had a good idea what John would say about that. Instead, trying not to look shamefaced, he said merely that Jane had overheard the scarred man talking in the gardens with Sir Miles, and had managed to get word out by Tom, who told Ben while he was walking Brutus. Finally, feeling rather empty, he told John he was sorry for keeping so much from him. Then he fell silent.

His master gazed at him for a long time, before drawing a deep breath. "I warned you, Ben," he said at last. "I asked you to forget all about that girl – and you agreed!"

Ben gave a nod, and lowered his eyes.

"Yet you defied me," John went on. "Instead, you went about asking questions… Why, Tom Slyte seems to know more about your doings than I do!" He looked more hurt than angry now. "What was it someone called you once?" he asked. "*The ferret*, wasn't it? The boy who can't resist ferreting about, no matter what scrapes he gets himself into!"

Although he kept his eyes lowered, Ben still had hopes. Despite all that had been said, he knew his master trusted him. He waited, while John looked down, unfolded the little square of parchment and stared at it.

"Is this all it is?" John asked, after a moment. "A few words – in Spanish, you say?"

"It came from Jane's uncle – he's a sailor," Ben said. "He must have found it on one of the ships he served on."

John sighed. "Well, what exactly was this 'word' Tom brought you?" he asked.

Ben told him what Jane had overheard when the man she knew as Perez had spoken with Sir Miles. But when he had finished, John merely shook his head.

"And you believed all that?" he demanded. "Does it not strike you that it might be just another tale – the workings of that girl's fevered imagination?"

Ben swallowed – then suddenly, he found his voice. "But it's true that Sir Miles has gone away in a hurry," he said. "Tom told me—"

"Sir Miles attends the Queen at Whitehall Palace, or so I've heard," John interrupted dryly. "He hasn't gone away, as gossips like Tom would have it. The man's getting married soon, have you forgotten that?"

He got to his feet and took a few paces about the room, before turning to face Ben. "I can't – nay, I *won't* take that girl's word," he said. "Though I can understand why, now you've put these scraps of information together, you think they make a clear picture. But have you not thought what it amounts to, Ben? Why, to my mind, it looks as if Jane is accusing Sir Miles Brandon of sending cannons to the Spanish – our sworn enemies! If that were true, it's not just treachery on Sir Miles's part – it's treason!"

Ben gulped. He knew that John was right: that was indeed what Jane had meant. How on earth had he become a part of all this? he wondered. He met John's eye, and saw how worried he was.

"Think carefully, Ben," his master went on. "These are terrible charges, the gravest you could make against any man – let alone one so powerful!"

Once again, doubts rose in Ben's mind. Had he got carried away by Jane's story? Had she merely woven a spell about him after all, as she had done about others – like the boy at Brandon Court, and perhaps even a man as hard-headed as Tom Slyte?

He pictured Jane again, and saw the look of desperation on her face, back in the gloomy storeroom at Brandon Court... Then finally he looked up at John.

"Yet I believe her," he said quietly. "I can't help it."

John stared at him. Then he drew a breath, went back to his chair and sat down. "You still don't understand," he said. "Even if every word of this were true, who would believe *you*?"

Outside, the rain still poured. Ben heard the footsteps of people hurrying past in the wet.

"But suppose even a part of it were true..." he began – then broke off as John shook his head.

"Who in all England would take the word of a boy player," he demanded, "or his master either, for that matter, if they were rash enough to accuse Sir Miles Brandon of something so terrible as high treason?"

"Lord Bonner would," Ben replied.

"His Lordship's gone from London," John told him. "He's in the country, I know not where. So whatever you or I do or don't do, we're on our own."

"But since we have proof," Ben began – then broke off as John threw up his hands.

"Proof?" he echoed. "A few words scrawled on a bit of parchment? Why, anyone could have done it! Couple this with wild accusations from the girl who tried to stab Sir Miles, plus the idle talk of a rat-catcher and a blacksmith, and what proof do you have?"

Seeing the look of dismay on Ben's face, John calmed himself.

"It's no use, Ben," he said. "If we took this to anyone with authority, we would be laughed at. We could be taken for madmen, and packed off to Bedlam!"

"Yet if we do nothing," Ben countered desperately, "and Sir Miles is really selling cannons to Spain..."

"I find that hard to believe," John said. "Too many people would know about it. Why, any sailor might talk—"

"But one did!" Ben exclaimed. "Jane's uncle found out, and told her father – and he didn't know who to tell either!"

"So she says," John repeated in a dry voice.

Ben knew that John had mistrusted Jane from the start. And after the lies she had told, and the way she had run away, he could hardly blame his master. There seemed little Ben could say to convince him. And yet...

"It's just..." He hesitated, but when John did not interrupt, he went on: "English cannons are the best, aren't they? And if our enemies could get their hands on them somehow, they'd do it, wouldn't they? And even if Sir Miles wasn't one of the wickedest men in England, as Jane says, we know how mean and greedy he is... And then there's the man with the scar – Perez, who spoke with an accent – I heard him myself! And he talked with Sir Miles about 'the goods' and 'the customer', so—"

"Enough!" John held up a hand in exasperation. "You should be a lawyer," he cried. "And if you'd been born a rich man's son, I'm sure one day you would become one!"

A sudden squall blew against the window, rattling the casement. John glanced outside. "Well, one thing's clear," he said, after a moment. "There will be no performance at the Curtain today."

Suddenly, Ben felt a surge of hope. His master had been doing his severe voice – and he was frowning again, which usually meant he was working something out. Trying not to raise his hopes, Ben waited.

"There's but one man I can think of whom I would dare to tell of this," John said at last. "Though he too may take offence..." He hesitated. "Yet he's wise and just, and doesn't despise players merely for what we are. Perhaps he would listen..." John stood up again, and looked gravely at Ben.

"Do you remember that day when I came to Hornsey village, to fetch you to London?" he asked. When Ben looked surprised, he went on: "And do you remember what I promised your mother? That you would not only learn the skills of a player, but you would be well cared for too, as one of my own family."

Ben nodded.

"Well – if I were to do what you wish, despite all my doubts, then I could be putting you in serious danger," John said. "For if the man I have in mind refuses to believe you – and worse, if Sir Miles gets to hear of it – you and I could both find ourselves charged with slander, and taken before a court. We could be pilloried, or branded, or even have our ears cut off. Do you understand that?"

Ben nodded again.

"Then I'll give you a choice," his master continued. "Do you still want to take your accusations against

Sir Miles to this man, and take whatever consequences may follow?"

"I think so," Ben mumbled. Then he drew himself up. "Yes," he said more loudly. "I do."

"Very well then!"

John had decided. He was no longer angry, Ben saw with relief. And if he was afraid himself, he hid it well.

"We'll go at once," he said, "rain or not."

When Ben stood up, he was a little shaky. "Where are we going?" he asked.

"To see Lord Walden."

Ben swallowed, but at once he knew that it was the right decision – perhaps the only one that John could make.

His master gave him a wry look. "But first you'd better take some breakfast," he said. "You look hungry enough to eat one of Slyte's dead rats!"

Ben and John trudged through the London streets, and both were soon dripping wet. Among the noisy, splashing crowds they walked, down Bishopsgate and along Three Needle Street to the Stocks Market. There they turned left into Walbrook, from where it was but a short walk to Dowgate, one of the narrow ways that led down to the Thames. Here, among the crowded tenements of poor folk, was a much larger building that took Ben by surprise: the town house of Lord Walden, with its fair garden and private landing stage on the riverside.

Ben was worried now. In fact, the longer he walked, the more worried he had become. He tried to concentrate on his "proof", as he still called it: the square of parchment, which he had placed in his purse. The rain had not let up, and he was so soaked now that he might as well have swum the river to get to Lord Walden's. Nervously he stood at John's side, as his master knocked on the door.

It was opened by a manservant in livery. At the sight of the two bedraggled figures, the fellow would have slammed the door, had not John told him they were servants of Lord Bonner, with a message for Lord Walden. Whereupon the man let them in, but left them in a passage while the rainwater ran from their clothes. It was some time before he came back and beckoned them to follow him.

They passed through rooms furnished with oak chests and wall hangings, to find themselves in a smaller chamber at the rear, overlooking the waterside. Outside, the rain still fell, yet boats could be seen plying back and forth. At sight of the figure seated by the window, John and Ben stopped in surprise and made their bows.

"My father is out," Lady Imogen Walden said. "He may return soon – or he may not. Will you deliver your message to me?"

John did not know what to say, while Ben felt very uneasy. There was a waiting-woman in an embroidered yellow gown standing behind Lady Imogen and looking curiously at him. Lady Imogen herself wore a simple cream-coloured gown, though there were jewels in her hair and pearls about her neck.

"It's a delicate matter, My Lady," John said at last. "I believe His Lordship would want to hear of it first."

The young woman regarded him with large brown eyes, then turned to Ben, who blushed. But at once she raised her eyebrows in surprise. "You're the boy who saved Sir Miles, at Brandon Court!" she exclaimed. "The hero of the day!"

Ben's colour deepened, from scarlet to a cherry-red that almost matched his doublet.

John spoke up. "My prentice Master Button, My Lady," he said. Not knowing what else to do, Ben bowed again.

The lady looked John up and down. "You're very wet," she said. "You could go to the kitchens and dry yourselves. The servants will give you a warm drink."

"Most kind, My Lady," John replied. "We'll go at once..."

But Lady Imogen raised a hand, heavy with jewelled rings. "First, I'd like to know the nature of this message," she murmured. And now Ben caught a look in her eye: the young woman was suspicious. "You say it's from your patron?"

John cleared his throat. "Not exactly," he answered. "It's...a matter of business, you might say."

"What sort of business?"

Standing next to John, Ben sensed his unease. Lady Imogen was watching him closely. Finally he said: "It concerns our company, My Lady. I...we were pleased that Lord Walden liked our performance at your betrothal feast. We beg to be allowed to play for him at some time in the future."

"Do you indeed?" Lady Imogen's face was blank. To Ben's eye, she looked quite different now from the smiling young bride-to-be he had last seen dancing with Sir Miles. There was a tautness about her mouth that spoke of a sulky nature behind the pretty face.

"Did you really walk here in the pouring rain, just to ask that?" Lady Imogen enquired. "Why did you not ask at Brandon Court, when my father spoke to you?"

John struggled to think of some explanation, but Ben was feeling quite miserable now. He recalled his master's words: *no matter what scrapes you get yourself into...* Only this time, he thought, he had got John into a scrape too – one that might end badly for them both.

"I'd like an answer," Lady Imogen said. "Or I might think you had some other reason for coming here."

John cleared his throat again. "My Lady..." he began, but the other interrupted him.

"Sir Miles told me you were not to be trusted," she snapped. "Players are thieves at heart, he says. Always looking for a chance to enrich themselves!"

Ben's heart was pounding. Beside him, John stood as stiff as a board.

"Your pardon, My Lady," he said. "Be assured I have the highest regard for you and for your father, and only wish you well. Perhaps I shouldn't have come here in such a manner. We'll take our leave—"

"Not yet you won't!" Lady Imogen stood up. She turned to her waiting-woman and spoke in a low voice. Then she faced the two players again.

"I think you came here for another reason," she said. "So what is it?"

Ben felt sweat breaking out on his brow. Suddenly, this young woman seemed as dangerous to him as did

Sir Miles and all his men-at-arms. How Ben and all of Lord Bonner's company had misjudged her, he thought – and at once, he was filled with alarm.

Could she know about Sir Miles's treachery – his dealings with England's enemies? If so, then she too would be guilty of treason! The idea made Ben go cold from head to foot. He shivered, and tried to hide it by looking out of the window – then he started, as a movement caught his eye.

His gaze went to the landing stage – and without thinking, he pointed. John, then Lady Imogen, turned to follow his outstretched finger – and saw Lord Walden himself, in a heavy fur-trimmed gown, being helped up the steps by a servant. Beyond, a waterman was pushing his oar against the jetty, sending his boat out onto the river. As they watched, His Lordship walked towards the house, the servant holding a cape above his head against the rain.

With a sigh of relief, Ben lowered his eyes. Now at last they would be able to speak with Lord Walden, instead of with his daughter. Although what that kindly old man might say when he heard such an unlikely tale, Ben had no idea.

But he was about to find out.

Chapter Sixteen

At first, when Lord Walden came into the room and saw John and Ben, he seemed pleased. He asked after Lord Bonner, and spoke again of how he had enjoyed the company's playing at Brandon Court. Then he turned to his daughter, who had risen to make her curtsy. But when he asked John what his business was, Lady Imogen interrupted her father, and said she must speak privately with him.

The young woman seemed flustered. And when Lord Walden said he would attend to the players first, her bottom lip quivered. But John met His Lordship's gaze, and the old man seemed to catch the urgency in his eye.

"I'll take Master Symes out to the stables," he said to Lady Imogen, "and show him your new Neapolitan horse." To John, he added: "It's a gift, from Sir Miles. I happen to know your patron has a mind to buy one, too – he'll be glad to have my opinion." He turned to his daughter again. "We'll talk when I return. Does that please you?"

Lady Imogen's eyes blazed, and her mouth was tight. She fingered the pearls at her neck, and for a moment Ben thought she would speak. But the waiting woman murmured in her ear...and at last, she made a stiff curtsy and sat down.

Once again, Ben breathed a sigh of relief. Soon he was following John and Lord Walden out through the rain, into a warm stable.

"There she is," His Lordship said. "Or did you think it was just an excuse to leave the house?"

He gestured to the nearest stall, where a trim little horse with a dark brown coat was eating hay from a manger. As Ben and his master came in, the animal raised a long, slender head and looked keenly at them.

"She's two years old," Lord Walden said. "The finest mare I've ever had in my stable – Sir Miles, as you know, is a man of good taste." The old man looked at John. "Yet even a horse such as this cannot talk – no matter what she may overhear."

John nodded, but Ben was feeling quite sick. He knew that, having come this far, he must tell His Lordship everything. Whether he believed Ben or not, it was too late to turn back.

"You have something important to say to me." His Lordship raised his brows. "Or am I mistaken?"

"With your leave, My Lord..." John seemed to summon his own courage. "I'll let my prentice tell you what he told me, but an hour ago. It's..." He hesitated. "It's quite a tale."

Lord Walden fixed his grey eyes upon Ben. "Then I would be most interested to hear it."

So Ben gave his account for the second time that day.

It was the same one he had given to John, though he left out a few things. He did not call Sir Miles the wickedest man in England, of course – nor did he accuse him of treason. But he did tell what he had learned from Jane. And when he had finished, he opened his purse and brought out the parchment.

"That's all I know, My Lord," he said, trying not to let his hand shake. "I swear it's true. And here are the words that Mistress Neale carried with her from Shropshire."

In the silence that followed, the horses could be heard stamping in their stalls. Lady Imogen's mare had lost interest in the visitors, and was finishing her meal. Finally, after what seemed an age, Lord Walden took the little square of vellum from Ben's hand. He was frowning, and Ben expected the worst – so he was surprised when the old man said: "As it happens, Sir Miles is not at Whitehall, as some believe. He's gone to his foundry in the west, on urgent business. One of his men came to fetch him. Although he promised to return in good time for the wedding."

Ben drew a sharp breath, as Lord Walden looked at the parchment with the scrawled words. Finally he looked up.

"So...*culebrina de hierro* means 'iron snake' in Spanish, does it? Intriguing...and a good nickname for a cannon, too."

The old man glanced towards the half-open door, and only now did Ben realize that the rain was no longer drumming on the stable roof. He looked out and saw ragged clouds scudding by and, in the distance, a shaft of pale sunlight.

"I've a mind to take some air by the waterside," His Lordship said to John. "Will you and your boy walk with me?"

And to the surprise of Ben and his master, he walked out.

Soon all three of them stood on the wet boards of his private jetty, with the noise of the city about them. And now, Lord Walden turned abruptly to John. "Do you know what risks you've taken, coming here like this?" he asked.

Stiffly, John answered that he believed he did.

"Yet still you came…" His Lordship's eyes shifted to Ben. And now, there seemed to be sadness in them. "Well – you're as brave and as sharp-witted a fellow as any I've met, Master Button," he said. "But you have no idea how your tale has chilled my blood. For I think you have made one mistake in your translation. It's slight – but it makes everything else clear."

The old man paused. "*Bretaña* does not mean 'Britain'," he said. "The Spanish call our land the *Reino de Inglaterra* – the Kingdom of England. *Bretaña* means 'Brittany'! That, as you may know, is in the north-west part of France, where the Spanish have had strongholds for years. Indeed, one of our greatest fears is that one day they may mount an invasion from there, across the English channel!"

Then, as Ben gasped and John's jaw dropped, His Lordship added: "So what you have told me, Master Button, makes complete sense – and suggests that the fears I and some of my fellow councillors have had are well founded. And in view of that, I might at last be able to take action – against the man who is set to become my own son-in-law. Yet if I do, it could mean the ruin not only of me, but of my own daughter too!"

The two players stood dumbfounded. From thinking he had not been believed, even fearing he might be arrested, Ben now saw that he had stumbled upon something bigger than he ever imagined. Here at last was the answer to the riddle: Sir Miles was shipping some of his "goods" from Bristol to Brittany – into the hands of England's enemy. His "customer" was none other than the King of Spain!

And Jane had been right all along – as Ben had been right to believe her. Sir Miles was indeed the wickedest of men – and what's more, he was guilty of high treason.

John spoke up anxiously. "My Lord – please remember that what my prentice has said is little more than hearsay," he said. "Though I trust him, I don't trust Jane Neale – I never have. I cannot be sure when she tells the truth, and when she lies. Indeed, I wonder whether she even knows it herself!"

But Lord Walden shook his head. "If it were only the testimony of that girl, Master Symes, I would

dismiss it," he said. "But there have been rumours...
vague ones, perhaps, but enough to alarm some –
even, as I said, men of the Queen's own council."

And as John looked stunned that what he had
thought a fanciful tale was turning out to be true, His
Lordship seemed to come to a decision.

"Whatever I will say here, I say in secret," he said.
"And you must both swear not to repeat a word as
long as you live! If you do, I'll deny what I've said
and have you arrested. So – do you agree?"

Ben's mouth was dry. He swallowed, waiting for
his master to speak first.

"I swear, My Lord," John murmured, and dropped
to one knee. He glanced at Ben, who quickly did the
same.

"I too swear, My Lord," he said.

"Very well." Lord Walden gestured to them both
to stand, then held the parchment out to Ben. "You
may take back this scrap that both you and the girl
have guarded so carefully, Master Button," he said.
"For by itself, it's worthless. Anyone could have
written it."

Ben took the parchment. Now he did not know
what to expect.

"I spoke of rumours, which have only lately
reached my ears," the old man went on thoughtfully.

"Yet the truth is, I refused to face them, for my daughter's sake. If only I had known more about the man she's set on marrying – for now I wish I had never set eyes on him!"

Lord Walden's distress was plain. To John and Ben, he looked less like an important member of the Queen's council, and more like a frail, careworn old man. And it seemed as if he was glad to speak, even to a humble player and his prentice. The two of them could only listen, and pity him in his plight.

"That man has turned Lady Imogen's head," he said gravely. "Ever since her mother died she's been a headstrong girl, who must be praised and flattered. When Sir Miles Brandon came to woo her, spoiling her with gifts, she was like a child being showered with dainties. By the time I saw how smitten she'd become, it was too late. He asked for her hand in marriage, and she begged me to give her approval, so I did." A look of anguish passed over his face. "And when Brandon asked me to put my consent in writing – merely to satisfy his lawyers, he said – I did that too! How foolish I was, I have come to realize – and I regret it bitterly!"

He broke off, gazing downstream towards London Bridge. "As I began to know that man better, I was dismayed," he went on. "And for the first time in my life, I would have gone back on my word, and withdrawn my consent – but I had put my seal to it! And in any case, as I should have known he would, Sir Miles forestalled me."

He put a hand to his brow. "There is a night that's burned on my memory," he said. "It was the night, not long ago, that Brandon came to this house and demanded to speak to me alone. And he told me plainly that if I ever tried to stop him marrying my daughter, he would swear out a warrant against me for breach of promise. He waved the document in my face, with my signature on it, and said he would ruin me. He would not rest until he had taken everything I had – down to my last candlestick, he said – and seen me thrown into a debtor's prison!"

The old man gave a bleak smile. "How long someone of my years could survive inside such a place, you may easily guess. And then what would become of my daughter? Headstrong she may be, but she's like a child in Brandon's hands. She knows little of his affairs, and refuses to hear a word against him." He sighed. "I knew it was no bluff on Sir Miles's part – for if any man in England has the will to carry out his threats, it's he. And more, he has the power and the money, too. For what that girl told you was true, Master Symes: in the western shires they call Brandon The Ironmaster, whose will cannot be resisted. Whatever he wants, he will have!"

Ben caught John's eye, and saw his dismay. As for Ben himself, he burned with anger against Sir Miles, his greed and his cruelty, as he pitied Lord Walden. Only one thing gave him a crumb of comfort: from His Lordship's words, he guessed now that Lady Imogen had no part in Sir Miles's treachery. It seemed that she knew nothing of what her husband-to-be was doing – she was just a vain and foolish young woman, who wanted to marry one of the richest men in England.

"Yet, do you know what the worst part is?" Lord Walden cried suddenly. "It's that Brandon has no real love for my daughter! It's not even her dowry he craves – for my own wealth is small compared with his. The man merely wants to join with one of England's oldest and noblest families, for the power and influence it will bring him. And I fear that soon Lady Imogen will regret her marriage to him – but by then it will be too late! He can treat her any way he likes!"

Ben and his master were silent. They understood Lord Walden's anguish: he faced losing everything – even his daughter. And so, without proof of Sir

Miles's wrongdoing, he had hesitated to act. Even the highest folk in the land, Ben thought, could meet their match.

"My Lord..." John struggled to find the words. "I'm sorry we came here, adding weight to your fears. If there were anything that could be done—"

But His Lordship broke in – and now Ben caught the gleam in his eye.

"An hour ago, I would have said there was nothing to be done," he said. "Yet you need not fret, John Symes – for you and your prentice have done right – and you have done more than you know."

He turned to Ben. "We suspected the cannons from Sir Miles's foundry didn't all reach our soldiers in Ireland – but we were not sure where they went. Now it seems clear to me – for you have supplied the missing piece to a puzzle, Master Button. And in doing so you have spurred me – nay, you have shamed me – to action!"

And Ben's heart lifted – for the old man's gloomy expression had faded, to be replaced by one of determination.

"The wedding is set to take place a week from today," he said, "at the church of St Olave. Now it's clear from the way Sir Miles hurried off that he went to speed dispatch of the 'goods'. So I and my fellow councillors must move as swiftly to collect evidence against him – enough, I hope, to put an end to The Ironmaster, and all his works!"

Hope surged through Ben. And seeing that John, too, was stirred, a thought flew to his mind – and before he could stop himself, the words were out.

"My Lord – I know you're a friend to our patron, Lord Bonner," he blurted, "so if you have need of assistance, will you trust one of his servants to help you?"

Lord Walden blinked in surprise. "What is it you think you can do?" he enquired.

Ben swallowed. "Well, I'm not quite sure yet," he began, then broke off as beside him John let out a groan. But quickly His Lordship spoke up.

"Well," he said, "I fear there's little someone like you can do. For what I need most is time – time to find the grounds to arrest Sir Miles, before he marries my daughter!" A worried frown creased his brow. "Yet whatever it takes, be it all of my strength as well as my wits, I will do it!"

He drew a breath. "Now you must go. I thank you for your offer of help – but remember: not a word of this to anyone!"

And with a final nod to John and Ben, he dismissed them both.

*

They walked back through the muddy, crowded streets. Ben glanced up at John, who was taking long strides, and saw his expression: one of exasperation. Finally he slowed down, and turned to Ben.

"What on earth were you thinking of?" he demanded. And before Ben could answer, he held up a hand. "Have you forgotten we're but common players, who can lose our place – even our liberty – at a moment's notice? We took a great risk going to His Lordship, and we've been mighty lucky!"

He shook his head, trying to calm down. "The doings of powerful noblemen are not our affair, Ben. Lord Walden may or may not have enough time to gather his evidence – but this affair is far too serious for you to meddle in it in any way. Now, do you understand?"

Ben kept quiet as they began walking again. Then finally he glanced up at John.

"Yes, I understand," he said. "But it won't stop me from thinking about it." He shrugged. "I'm sorry – but I can't help it."

John threw him one of his "severe" looks, and strode on.

Chapter Seventeen

*A*pril gave way to May. The week leading up to Sir Miles's wedding passed in a flurry of performing and rehearsing, but, for Ben, little changed. The only news that interested him was when he met Tom Slyte in the street, and heard that Jane was gone from Brandon Court. The girl's stepfather had ridden from Shropshire and taken her away.

It left Ben with an empty feeling. For the strange thing was that, despite everything, he missed Jane. He missed her green eyes and her fierce temper, and her strength of will. Yet the fact remained that all her efforts to bring Sir Miles Brandon to justice had likely been in vain. For it seemed as if no proof existed of Sir Miles's treachery – and as far as anyone knew, none ever had. What Lord Walden and his fellow councillors were doing to collect evidence, Ben had no idea. But it worried him, for if none were found in time, he knew the wedding would go ahead – and Lady Imogen Walden would become Lady Brandon. The Ironmaster, it seemed, could still do as he pleased – and get away with it.

Each day Ben went to his work at the Curtain. He did his chores, practised his lute and walked Brutus, but the whole time the cruel injustice of the matter weighed upon him. Yet there was no one he could talk to. Tom Slyte had finished catching rats at Brandon Court and gone elsewhere. Ned Campion's hammer still rang through the street, but there was nothing Ben could say to Ned. Even Harry Higgs had moved across the river, so there were no puppets to divert the young folk of Shoreditch.

But the worst thing was that Ben could not tell the rest of Lord Bonner's Men what he knew – even Matt. He and John had been sworn to secrecy by Lord Walden, and were bound by their promise. And John, it seemed, was trying to forget the whole business. There was nothing they could do, he told Ben, and he should look to his work. Now everyone was talking of the Whitsun Ale, less than a week away. Practising songs and dances kept the company busy, which was how John liked it.

And that was how things stood, until Ben woke up on the following Tuesday morning, and remembered that it was the day of the wedding.

News of the forthcoming event was all around Shoreditch, of course, as it was all over London. This time Lord Bonner's Men had not been invited to play, despite Ben saving Sir Miles's life. It was typical of the man's meanness, the players said, not to mention his ingratitude – although Ben, who now knew more about Sir Miles than any of them did, was not surprised. If only there was real proof of his wicked deeds, Ben thought... Then all at once, he knew what he must do.

Ever since he had made his offer of help to Lord Walden, he had wondered how he might carry it out. Now, an idea sprang to his mind with crystal clarity. Since it looked as though no one else was going to do it, he would have to stop Sir Miles's wedding himself!

Feeling scared, Ben sat up on his pallet. He had been in scrapes before, but nothing quite like this. The consequences...well, he refused to think about them. For even if he was the boy who had saved Sir Miles's life, somehow he didn't think that would matter much if he were arrested and thrown into prison. And whether he were branded, or had his ears cut off, the outcome would be the same: he would be finished as a boy player.

Feverishly, he got up to get dressed. He was shivering, and not from the draught that came down the chimney. It was because, very soon, he began to have doubts.

Could he really do such a thing on his own? A mere prentice – indeed anyone who wasn't invited to the wedding – would not be allowed near Sir Miles, let alone in the church. His men were always near – at the first sign of an intruder they would pounce. The notion looked hopeless, as well as foolish. Yet Ben drew a breath, and told himself that if he did nothing, he would regret it for the rest of his days.

But a plan was forming in his mind that gave him hope. Of course he had no powers, and no rights at all – but there was one thing he did have, which had served him well enough: his skill as a player. And now, perhaps, that skill should be put to the test, as it had never been before.

Fully dressed, afraid but determined, he went downstairs.

There were sounds from the kitchen, and Ben tensed; he did not want to see Alice, for he knew he could not lie to her. He stepped across the passage to the street door – but then Brutus trotted up, thinking it was time for his walk. Ben's heart sank.

"Not now!" he whispered, and tried to shoo the old hound away – but Brutus did not understand. There was nothing for it: Ben opened the door to slip through, just as Alice appeared.

"Where are you going?" she asked sharply.

Ben gulped. "To church," he said, and hurried out.

St Olave's was a small church on the corner of Hart Street and Sidon Lane, just below Tower Hill. Already that morning, a crowd had gathered outside. They were ordinary folk, some in their best clothes, who had come to watch the wedding procession arrive. The day was fair, with a light breeze. Sir Miles and his bride were expected soon, and people stood in the sunshine, gossiping. It seemed the couple would not exchange vows outside the church, as some did, but inside. The parson was already waiting. After the ceremony the party would walk back to Sir Miles's grand house nearby, where feasting would begin. So many noblemen and women were invited, it would be like a Royal Progress in the parish!

After a while, a scent of perfume drifted towards the onlookers. Heads turned to see a young woman walking down the street, dressed in an elaborate pink gown and a hat trimmed with fine lace. Below the hat fell a mass of golden curls, framing a face painted heavily with make-up. A murmur rose: surely this was one of Sir Miles's guests? In which case, the wedding party could not be long.

Of course, none of the watchers knew what turmoil the face concealed, or how much perspiring was going on under the golden wig. But then, most people in Ben Button's place would have been trembling from head to foot!

Ben halted before the church door, trying to look as if he had every right to be there. His main fear was not that someone would recognize him under the make-up, but that they would recognize the clothes. For his costume was none other than the one he wore as Delia in *The Old Wives' Tale*.

It had taken him over an hour to get ready, alone in the tiring room of the Curtain, with no Will to help him dress. Luckily the main doors had been unlocked, for some hired men were there, practising a scene. They took no notice when Ben came in, whistling casually, nor when he disappeared behind the stage.

What worried him, once he had struggled into his costume, was how to get outside without being seen. No one was allowed to take costumes out of the theatre – they were too valuable. So, after checking his make-up in a looking glass, Ben waited, peering through a crack in the door. His chance came when the hirelings stopped to discuss a line that was causing difficulties. As they gathered at one side of the stage, arguing amongst themselves, Ben slipped out onto the other side of the stage and hurried down the steps. Then, to his relief, he was soon across the yard and through the entrance. After that he had merely walked down to Bishopsgate, ignoring the curious glances of passers-by, and round the outside of the walls, before turning into the city through Aldgate.

His plan was not merely bold – it was so risky it made him feel weak in the stomach. But he had been unable to come up with a better one. He had offered to help Lord Walden – and he must do what he could, whatever John might say. Delia's costume was the best disguise he could think of, and the only one that might get him inside the church. After that he would say his piece – and trust to luck.

So there he stood, wearing a lofty expression and trying to imagine that he was at the Curtain giving a performance. After all, he was a player, wasn't he? Although the old stone church was as unlike a theatre as anywhere he knew...

Excited cries broke out, and his heart thudded like Ned Campion's hammer. "Sir Miles! Here he comes!"

Ben turned to look. For a moment it was like that Sunday in Bishopsgate Street, with bystanders gaping as Sir Miles and his men rode past, their trappings shining in the sunlight. Again he caught the flash of silks and jewels, as the splendidly dressed group drew near. He saw Sir Miles and, walking beside him, Lady Imogen in a silver gown. Then he was almost knocked off his feet as people surged forward. Some shouted blessings upon Sir Miles and his bride as the party approached the church door. When they drew near to Ben, he had a sudden panic: his disguise might not be enough to fool Sir Miles or Lady Imogen. So he did the only thing he could think of: dropped to a curtsy, and bowed his head.

It worked! With barely a glance at him, Sir Miles swept by towards the arched doorway. By the time Ben looked up again, all he could see were the backs of people disappearing into the church. So, taking a deep breath, he raised himself to his full height, detached himself from the onlookers and followed the guests. He tried to ignore Sir Miles's servants, two of whom had appeared from somewhere to man the doors. But as Ben started to enter the church, one of the men raised a hand, barring his entry. The other took hold of the heavy door and was about to close it, shutting him out.

There was no time to waste. Ben had one chance, and a poor one at that – but he must take it.

"How dare you, fellow!" he demanded, in the most haughty voice he could manage. "I've come all the way from…from Bristol, to attend the wedding of my kinsman. Do you refuse me? I assure you, Sir Miles will be most angry when he hears of it!"

The guards had been looking suspiciously at him, but now they were uneasy. This guest was unexpected, yet she appeared to be a high-born young lady, richly dressed and well spoken. Finally, the one who was holding the door spoke.

"You're related to Sir Miles, madam?"

"I am," Ben replied. "Third cousin on his mother's side – do you wish to hear my family history? I fear it will take some time…"

But his boldness was rewarded, for the man stepped back. "No need, My Lady," he said hastily. "You should hurry – they're about to begin." He bowed, as did his companion. So, without a backward glance at them, Ben went into the church.

At once he was surprised by the size of the crowd. He realized that there had been guests inside, awaiting the wedding party. The little church was crammed full, with people crushed to the back behind the rear pews. Ben felt the heat of bodies in heavy clothes, and the excitement in the air. To his alarm, he also noticed some of Sir Miles's men standing by the walls. But the aisle – his only getaway – was clear. Already the betrothed couple had moved down it, to stand before the old priest in his cassock. Then Ben realized that one important person was not there: the bride's father, Lord Walden. Clearly he had not returned to London in time – which gave Ben some measure of comfort. It indeed rested on him to stop the marriage after all.

And already people were hushing their neighbours. With pulse racing, Ben heard the parson speak. He could barely make out what he said, but it hardly mattered, for the marriage service was short. Soon Sir Miles would speak the words: *I, Miles, take thee, Imogen, to my wedded wife, for better or worse, and thereto I plight my troth...* Then when Lady Imogen had made her vow, it would all be over. He must act now – or give up the whole plan.

There was nothing between him and The Ironmaster except the stone-flagged aisle. Drawing on every scrap of his courage, Ben walked down it between the rows of pews. He was aware of a stir from all sides. People looked round, pointing at him – and then disaster struck. A voice rang out – and at once several of Sir Miles's men sprang forward, to force their way through the crowded pews. Someone called to Ben to stop there and not take another step!

But Ben didn't stop. While voices rose about him, he kept walking, until he was but a few feet away from the bride and bridegroom, who turned around in surprise. Then he halted, and called out as loudly as he could.

"Stop! The marriage must not take place!"

There was silence, followed by a gasp of astonishment.

"It cannot go ahead," Ben went on, struggling to keep his voice from shaking, "for Sir Miles Brandon is already betrothed – to me!"

There were cries of dismay. But with heart pounding, Ben stood his ground, unsure what to say next. For one odd moment he wondered what the consequences might be for telling a lie in church. But then his attention flew to the person he had no wish to hurt – and who was most shocked of all.

Lady Imogen was staring at him in horror. The posy of flowers she had been holding dropped from her hand, and the hand went to her mouth. But almost at once another voice broke in.

"Sir Miles...can this be true?"

It was the parson. Now that Ben was closer, he saw that he was a stout old man, with sharp eyes beneath bushy white brows. His expression was stern as he gazed at Sir Miles – then quickly he shifted it to Ben.

"Who are you, madam?" he asked. "You have made a grave charge – I pray you, state your name!"

Suddenly Ben was tempted to throw all hopes of escape aside, and accuse Sir Miles outright. He could hardly be in more trouble, he thought, no matter what he did. But instead he swallowed, and said: "My name matters little, sir. I was compelled to come here, for justice's sake. Please believe me when I say it would be a mistake to let the wedding proceed!"

The parson frowned. "You said Sir Miles was betrothed to you," he argued. "I demand that you give your name and show me the evidence, otherwise—"

"There is no evidence!"

Sir Miles almost spat the words, silencing not just the priest but the entire congregation. As always, The Ironmaster was recovering quickly. With eyes blazing, he stared at Ben.

"I've never set eyes on this woman!" he shouted. "She's lying! I am not betrothed – and never have been. As for her name..." He swung his gaze to the parson. "I swear to you I will find that out – as I will find out who has sent her here, and why!"

Awkwardly, he faced Lady Imogen. "It's a lie, My Lady," he said. "Doubtless she's been sent by one of my enemies, to try and spoil our happiness. Be assured, I will get to the bottom of it!"

Impatiently he turned to the parson again. "You have my word that there's nothing to stop my bride and I from taking our wedding vows!" he snapped. "Please proceed!"

But there was confusion now. All over the church, voices were raised, mingled with cries of alarm as the first of Sir Miles's men squeezed their way through into the aisle. Two or three of them hurried up behind Ben, blocking his escape. But before they could arrest him, the parson's voice rose above the din.

"Stay yourselves!" he cried. And as the servants stopped in their tracks, the old man raised a forbidding hand. "This is a holy place – none shall defile it!"

Then, fixing Sir Miles with a clear eye, he added: "Sir, I cannot proceed until I am certain. Any man – or woman – who objects to a service of marriage must be heard, until truth is satisfied. Otherwise, your vows may be worthless!"

Sir Miles drew breath, biting back a harsh reply. Instead he whirled on Ben – and it took all Ben's strength of will not to step back. Now voices dropped, as everyone stared at the two unlikeliest opponents they had ever seen. One was a golden-haired young woman, short of stature, in a pink gown. Towering over her was Sir Miles Brandon, hands clenched at his sides as if he wished to grasp his accuser by the throat. Sparks seemed to fly from his eyes – then all at once, recognition dawned on his face – and Ben's illusion was shattered.

"This is no woman! He's a boy!"

There was a gasp from every throat. For Ben, the world appeared to stand still. He wanted to run, but his legs wouldn't work. He had time to wonder if this was the most foolish thing he had ever done in his life, and decided it was. Earlier that morning, his plan had been to denounce Sir Miles as a man who had already promised to marry another – then get himself out of the church as quickly as he could. The wedding would have to be stopped until he had been found and questioned – but by then Ben would be away somewhere, getting out of his costume. When he next appeared, it would be as any boy in the street, curious to know what had happened. He might even have joined in the hue and cry for the mysterious woman who had fled the church...

But of course, it had not turned out that way at all! Now he blinked, as Sir Miles's hand flew up to tear the hat and wig from his head, revealing Ben's own tousled hair beneath. Of course Sir Miles knew him – how could Ben have thought he wouldn't? The knight's face seemed to fill the air before him, as a look of triumph came over it. Behind, Ben was dimly aware of the parson and Lady Imogen staring at him...then:

"Seize him!" Sir Miles shouted. Strong arms took hold of Ben – as they had done that day in the pavilion when he had jumped from the stage to save Sir Miles from Jane. But this time he was the one caught – and he would stay caught.

Noise filled the church. There were shouts, even screams. Those nearest to Ben were on their feet, as if fearing what would happen next. But even as the guests drew back, Sir Miles turned to them, eager to stop the disruption to his wedding.

"Hear me!" he shouted. "The boy is crazed! I know him – he tried to attack me once! Please stay where you are – there's no reason to be afraid. My men will take him away, and all will be well!"

Sir Miles's servants were crowding into the aisle. But before they could drag Ben off, the knight leaned forward and pushed his face close to him, so that no one else could hear. His expression was one of blind fury, as he took Ben by the forearm and gripped it savagely.

"You'll die for this," he hissed. "And your master too!"

Ben felt dizzy. He smelled strong drink on Sir Miles's breath, as pain shot through his arm. Vaguely he was aware of his Delia hat and wig lying on the stone floor. Sir Miles's fingers, with their many rings, bit into his flesh. His wrists were wrenched back, so hard he thought his bones would break. And all the while he was aware of the crowd, their voices swirling about him like smoke. Any moment now, he thought, he would fall into a faint – and no one would help him. He had challenged Sir Miles, and lost. What a fool he had been, to think he could do anything else. He had failed.

Then he froze, as a clear voice sounded from somewhere behind him.

"Release the boy – in the Queen's name!"

Dazedly, Ben tried to look round. He heard muttering from the guards, and saw their looks of surprise. But they were as nothing to the black glare upon Sir Miles's face as he whirled about, looking for the man who had spoken. Then even he faltered – but Ben's heart leaped, as his arms were freed. And his relief was such that he thought he might faint after all.

For there was no mistake: Lord Walden, in his black gown and gold chain of office, had arrived at last! In a dignified manner, he walked down the aisle. Behind him came others – noblemen, by their appearance – and behind them were men-at-arms carrying halberds.

"Stand aside!" His Lordship cried, in a voice of such command that Sir Miles's men fell back. To their amazement, Lord Walden raised a hand and pointed at their master.

"I am a peer of the realm, and a member of the Queen's council. Sir Miles Brandon, I arrest you in the Queen's Majesty's name, and charge you to obey me!"

Then, as onlookers gasped, he addressed the guards again. "If any man resists me," he announced, "he too will be charged, on pain of death!"

As one, the terrified men dropped to their knees. But Lord Walden ignored them, and turned instead to the congregation. "Make way!" he cried. "This man will be taken to the Tower, to await the Queen's pleasure!"

For a moment, silence fell again – then Ben saw something he would never have thought possible.

Sir Miles staggered backwards and put a hand to his forehead, the colour draining from his face. But at once the silence was shattered, as a terrible scream rang out – and all eyes flew to Lady Imogen Walden.

The young woman was staring wild-eyed at her father and her husband-to-be. There, in front of everyone, she screamed again, a cry of anguish and rage, before sinking to her knees in her silver bridal gown and bursting into tears.

And in spite of everything, Ben felt only pity for her. Foolish and spoiled Lady Imogen may have been – but she did not deserve to ruin her life by marrying one of the wickedest men in England.

Rubbing his sore arm, Ben looked around. Sir Miles was being escorted through the crowd, surrounded by Lord Walden's guards. And suddenly, his own servants seemed to be melting away. People were hurrying from the church, talking excitedly, no doubt to see the prisoner marched off.

For that was what he was: a prisoner. Ben could hardly believe what had happened. In that moment, he found himself gazing into the grey eyes of Lord Walden. He dropped to one knee, but His Lordship took Ben's hand, and raised him to his feet.

Stooping, he picked up Ben's hat and wig and handed them to him. "You had better take these, Master Button," he said quietly. "I'm sure you gave quite a performance – but perhaps it's one you would rather forget?"

Ben murmured his thanks. His dangerous bluff had failed – but it had served its purpose. In the few precious minutes it had bought, Lord Walden and his fellows had been hurrying to St Olave's to arrest Sir Miles, before Lady Imogen could make her vows. Still somewhat shaky, he listened as His Lordship spoke again.

"Does your master know what you have done here?" he asked. And when Ben merely shook his head, he went on: "I thought so. Well, you may tell him you have my approval – not to mention my thanks. I will send word to John Symes when I may..." The old man glanced around. "For the moment, I have other things to attend to. But as for you, master player, I think it's best you go back to the theatre and return that costume. Don't you?"

And Ben's heart warmed as the old man's face creased in a smile. Weakly, he nodded, and breathed a sigh.

Now at last, he thought, it was really over.

Chapter Eighteen

The following Sunday was the seventh after Easter – the day of Pentecost. It was the day of the Whitsun Ale, which the whole of Shoreditch had looked forward to for weeks. It was also a day Ben Button would not forget, for something happened that he could never have expected. And it came about because of Harry Higgs.

It was a sunny spring day, with May blossom everywhere. The field behind St Leonard's church was alive with colour, as the parish folk gathered in celebration. And while it may not have rivalled the splendour of Brandon Court, there was a lot more fun and laughter about, which grew as the day wore on.

In the Symes house things got off to an edgy start, with Kate and Meg too excited to eat breakfast. And though Alice scolded and John tried his severe voice, they knew it was useless. So the girls were allowed to join their friends, who were already hurrying up Bishopsgate Street towards the church. For his part, Ben was thoughtful. Although he looked forward to performing – even to seeing Master Higgs and his puppets again – so much had happened in the past days that he was still taking it all in.

The most important news was that Sir Miles Brandon had been tried by the Queen's council, and would be executed on Tower Hill. Imprisoned with him was his steward, Nicholas Sparrow. Whispering Nick, it turned out, had tried to flee after Sir Miles's arrest. He disguised himself and might well have got away, but unluckily for him he could not disguise his voice. He was caught by the Aldgate bar – the limit of city authority, at the east border of London – and taken to the Tower to join his master.

After that Ben heard nothing until John Symes was called to Lord Walden's house, and came back with startling news. In the days after Ben and John had gone to Lord Walden with Jane's accusations, events had moved more swiftly than they knew. By order of the Queen, soldiers had ridden fast to Bristol – in time to halt a large shipment of cannons from Sir Miles's ironworks.

Hidden down the barrel of one of the cannons, the soldiers discovered documents, written in both English and Spanish, which revealed everything. The guns were to go to Cork harbour in Southern Ireland, where they would be unloaded, and the ships sent back to England. Then, unknown to the English, other ships without flags came by night to take the cannons away south to the Spanish-held ports in Brittany. Jane's sailor uncle must have somehow stumbled upon the documents, and torn off an important fragment, which had found its way to Jane. It was a matter of great relief to Ben to find that she had been right all along: the guns had been bound for the Spanish.

The Queen's soldiers also found Sir Miles's overseer, a Portuguese, but this man proved less easy to capture than his master. He had fought hard, wounding two men with his sword, before meeting his match. There on the Bristol quayside he had died, his blood spilling on the cold stones. Ben still felt a shiver when he remembered the scarred man on his tall horse, with the hard eyes that bored into his.

Now that all was known, the Queen had closed down Sir Miles's foundry, and was making plans for a fleet to attack the Spanish harbours. The new Armada, if there was to be one, was doomed before it had even sailed.

It shook John Symes so much when he heard the story that he could not be angry with Ben for disobeying him and taking such risks, let alone for borrowing a costume. In fact, he was more proud of him than he could say – but he could tell no one about it. For the truth was, both Ben and John were still sworn to secrecy by Lord Walden. Brandon's treason was a fearful business, which could spread fear and unrest throughout England, His Lordship said. The details would be kept quiet. And in a way, Ben was relieved by that, for he had no wish to tell the tale again. Although part of him could hardly believe that he had helped to save the nation from danger, another part of him was simply glad that it was all over. At last he could put heart and mind into what he loved best: performing with Lord Bonner's Men.

There was one thing John could tell the company: Lord Walden had sent a reward – a purse of gold sovereigns. He said it was to make up for the small payment they got from Sir Miles for playing at

Brandon Court, though Ben and John knew better: that it was in return for Ben preventing his daughter's marriage, and restoring her to him.

John had to fend off one or two puzzled questions from the players. The payment was large because His Lordship was a generous man, he said. So Will could stop grumbling now, and have some new costumes made for Ben and Matt. The company could also get a playmaker to pen them a new play. Why, they might even persuade Master Shakespeare to write for them...which set everyone talking. Ben and John had exchanged relieved looks when the questions ceased.

So it was that, although all of London knew that Sir Miles Brandon would be executed, few knew the true reasons behind it. Even fewer pitied the man: he was hard and cruel, folk said, and must have been up to no good. Yet privately, Ben did not like to think of Sir Miles's head ending up on a pike above the gatehouse of London Bridge, where those executed for the worst crimes were displayed. Luckily, Ben had no need to cross the river – and he hoped it would be a long time before he did.

Within an hour of rising that bright May morning, he had left the house with John, and in the sunshine his spirits soon lifted. Alice would follow later with Brutus. The street was thronged with excited folk, all heading for St Leonard's. But Ben was still surprised, when they reached the churchyard, to see how big the crowd was. It could rival the great St Bartholomew's Fair, he thought, though he had never seen it himself. Since it took place in summer, he always seemed to be away...

"Here at last!" Solomon Tree appeared, glum-faced, with his drum on a cord around his neck. "Folk are getting restless – they want music, which means us." He nodded towards the field, where a low stage was set up. "At least we won't have to do anything dangerous."

Ben saw a juggler, throwing balls in the air. Beyond him was a fire-eater, taking flaming wands into his mouth and bringing them out smoking, while people gazed in wonder.

John tapped his lute, which was on his back in its leather case. "We'll give them something else to cheer them," he said. And without further ado, Ben followed John and Solomon to join their fellows. A few minutes later, to cheers and applause, Lord Bonner's Men began a lively jig, while a crowd surrounded the stage. Now at last Ben's heart swelled, and his cares of the past weeks faded. He threw a grin at Matt, who was red-faced as he blew upon his hautboy, and got a nod in return. He smiled at Hugh and Gabriel with their recorders. Solomon was beating his tabor, while he and John plucked away at their lutes. Already people were dancing. Nearby, children had formed a ring and were skipping round to the music.

Will Sanders arrived, pushing his way through the dancers. Under one arm he held a keg of ale, while from his other hand dangled several mugs. He stopped in front of the players and grinned, whereupon for some reason the music speeded up. It would be a good day now – Ben felt it in his bones. But quite how it would turn out, he could not have guessed.

They played, and they danced, and stopped to take a drink, then played again. Jigs and hornpipes flew by, as did the songs they had practised. In no time, the morning was gone and the sun was warm overhead. Ben's fingers were sore again, and sweat ran down his face. He had lost count of the folk who had passed by the stage and greeted him. Tom Slyte was there, without his pole, but with Peascod on the leash. Ned Campion, with Squeaky Martin in tow, wandered through, greeting folk he knew, which meant all of Shoreditch. Alice, Kate and Meg had stayed to clap along with the music, before going to join in the games. The stalls selling gingerbread and pies were busy, while in Shoreditch Street, in front of the church, morris men were dancing, with a hobby horse weaving among them. Ale was in good supply, though for a while it was rumoured that the church wardens were running out of their specially brewed stock. But then the landlord of the Squirrel Inn appeared, wheeling a barrow with kegs on it. The fair began to roar – and it would not stop until late that night.

But it was in the afternoon that an incident took place which at first looked troubling. In the end, however, it would only add spice to the day – as well as providing the wags of Shoreditch with jokes for years to come.

Lord Bonner's players had eaten dinner, and were taking a rest before going back to the stage. From the street they could hear the bells of the morris men, and some of them went out to watch. But Ben and Matt stayed, for at one side of the field, by a hedge, stood Harry Higgs's theatre. The puppet man was ready to give his show.

The players had seen him arrive, leading his old mule, its back piled with baggage under the familiar red and green tent cover. But since the dinner at the White Hart, when they and the puppet master had put aside their differences, there was no ill feeling. Even Will greeted Higgs as he made his way across the field, gathering a trail of excited children behind him. The puppet master, as usual, swept off his hat and flashed a smile at Lord Bonner's Men from under his moustache. The one thing that surprised them was that Higgs seemed to have gained a helper – a boy dressed as he was, in striped breeches and bright yellow doublet, topped off with a wide-brimmed hat. From a distance, Ben had watched the lad scurry about, unpacking the mule and setting up the tent. And he was pleased to think that Master Higgs, whom he had seen in pain that day in Finsbury Fields, had found someone to do the heavier tasks, leaving him free to do what he did best: work his puppets.

Ben and Matt walked over to stand at the back of Higgs's crowd. Kate and Meg were in front, seated on the grass. Nearby sat Squeaky Martin, eating gingerbread. And no sooner had they arrived than there came a flourish on a tin trumpet, and a shout went up. Two puppets appeared on the little stage, and the play began.

The trumpet had been sounded by Higgs's helper, standing beside the little theatre. He then hurried round the back to help his master, though Ben knew it was Master Higgs doing the voices. The play was *Gawain and the Green Knight* again, and in spite of having seen it often, Ben was soon enjoying the action.

Beside him, Matt sniggered. "You're still an infant at heart," he said, "no matter how many women's parts you play!"

"Then why do you stay, if you're so grown-up?" Ben retorted.

Matt shrugged. But he stayed until the end, and joined in the applause when the puppets took their bows. Higgs appeared from behind the tent, but this time it was the boy who came out to take the money. And this time, perhaps because everyone was in such good spirits, the crowd did not melt away. Soon coins were clinking in the bowl he held, and the collection grew quickly. Ben felt for his purse and drew out a halfpenny. He looked round for Matt, but his fellow player had vanished.

"Skinflint," Ben muttered. He turned back as Harry Higgs's helper drew near – and froze. At once, he realized that all along there had been something familiar about the boy – and now, he saw what it was:

From under the brim of the hat, Jane Neale's green eyes stared back at him!

Neither of them spoke – until Jane grabbed him by the arm and leaned close. "You won't give me away," she said. "I know you won't!"

Ben gazed at her – and knew why he had not

recognized the girl sooner. It was not her clothing, but the change in her face. The strain and bitterness, the wild look in her eyes – all were gone. She looked like a smooth-faced boy, content in his work, who hated no one.

"Come – let me explain," she whispered. "I owe you that, and more..." She even smiled. "I know about The Ironmaster – as I heard about the boy who acted so bravely in the church, and stopped his wedding!" There was a glow in Jane's eyes, of gratitude mixed with admiration. She let go of Ben's arm. "There's justice after all," she went on. "You first knew me as a beggar – and now thanks to you, this beggar has had her revenge!"

Ben was astounded – especially when Jane hurried off round the back of the puppet theatre, indicating that Ben should follow. He did so, and found a gap in the hedge, with Jane squeezing herself through it. Ben did the same – and as soon as they were out of sight, she turned to him.

"Before you think ill of me, I swear I've done no wrong," she said. "Please believe me, for I've no reason to lie now." She smiled again. "I haven't lied to Master Higgs – he knows my story. He's a good man, kinder than people think. He's teaching me all he knows, so that one day I can take over his theatre.

I'll be like the son he once had, who died when he was small." She drew a breath, and looked grave. "As Harry Higgs is like the father I lost."

So many questions flooded into Ben's mind, he hardly knew where to begin. "I heard your stepfather came to take you home," he began, whereupon Jane nodded.

"I ran away, before we'd even travelled a mile. It was easy to lose him in London. He's a simple countryman – but a good husband to my mother. He will raise my brothers and sisters well. It's I who cannot stay there – my old life disappeared when my father died." She sighed. "I can't go back, Ben. I've grown to like the ways of travelling folk."

But soon she was smiling again. "I crossed the river," she went on, "and on Bankside I found Master Higgs, and befriended him. I knew my life had changed – as he knew I was the one to learn his craft. I love his puppets – they're like a family to us. Besides, Higgs has promised we'll go to Shropshire one day. Then I can see my real family, and make my peace with them."

Slowly, Ben nodded. He saw a light in Jane's eyes – not the light of anger, which she had shown at Hog Lane, but the light of happiness – something he had never thought to see in this girl.

"Then I can only wish you well," he said at last. "Now I should go, or my master will wonder what I do."

But before he could leave, Jane stayed him. "I never told you," she said, "but I'd have liked nothing more than to be a player like you. But since only boys can go on the stage, this will have to be enough."

It was Ben's turn to smile. "So, what shall I call you – *master*?" he asked.

"Tobias, of course," Jane answered. "What do you think?"

Then she startled him by kissing him on the cheek – twice. "One is for Kate and Meg," she said, "the other's for John and Alice. They're not for you – even if you are a true hero, whom I will always admire."

Then she stood aside, and waited while he climbed back through the hedge.

Ben walked past the puppet theatre in a daze. Harry Higgs was rummaging in his props basket, and looked up. "Master Button..." He stood up stiffly, and nodded.

Ben gave his greeting, but did not mean to stay. He did not think Master Higgs would like him sharing Jane's secret. And when Jane herself appeared, straightening her clothing after a tussle with the hedge, he started to move off – when a voice sounded from behind that set his teeth on edge.

"You! Now what mischief are ye up to?"

Ben turned, to find himself face-to-face with James Plugg.

"No mischief," he answered. "I came to see my friend Master Higgs – now I must get back to my company..."

But before he could take a step, the constable grabbed him by his collar. "Ye don't walk away from me until I say so," he growled. "And where's that other young rogue – the one who throws fits?"

Taking hold of Plugg's arm, Ben tried to pull it away. "This is a new shirt," he said. "My master will be angry—"

Suddenly Plugg let go – and Ben saw why: his eyes had fallen on Jane. And only then did Ben remember that she was not only the girl who had once given Plugg the slip, disguised as a beggar – she was also the one who tried to stab Sir Miles Brandon. If Plugg arrested her, she would be finished!

"I know you, boy." The constable glowered at Jane. "I never forget faces...just give me time, and I'll remember!"

Jane stiffened – but quickly a figure stepped

forward to stand between her and Plugg. Harry Higgs wore his broad smile, but those who knew him well would have been wary. He raised a hand – and on it was the dragon puppet.

"What does it matter to you, fat-guts?" the dragon snarled. "Tobias here is a hard-working prentice. Leave him alone, or I'll singe your eyebrows!"

There was laughter – a crowd was gathering. Plugg scowled, while Master Higgs as usual wagged a finger at the dragon.

"That's enough," he said sternly. "The constable here is only doing his duty—"

He broke off as a hand shot out. In a trice the constable had snatched the puppet off Higgs's hand and thrown it to the ground. People muttered angrily – but the children gasped.

"I left you alone last time you came here," Plugg growled, glowering at the puppet master. "But no one talks to James Plugg like that – seems to me you could do with a touch of the lash!"

There was a groan from the onlookers. Ben looked round desperately, trying to think what to do – when all at once there was a stir, as a bulky shape emerged from the crowd.

"No he couldn't," Ned Campion said. "And it seems to *me* you're a mite too free with that lash of yours, Master Plugg. Maybe it's time someone taught *you* a lesson!"

Plugg turned angrily – but immediately there was a loud crack, followed by a gasp as the constable staggered backwards. Ned's beefy fist had connected with his nose – a thunderous blow that shook him from head to toe. Plugg blew out a great breath, like Ned's bellows. Then, with blood running from his nose, he sat down heavily on the grass, staring stupidly up at the blacksmith.

"Bravo!" Tom Slyte was there with Peascod. "Ned, you'd make a better constable! Would he not?" the rat-catcher cried, appealing to the crowd. Without hesitation, they shouted back.

"He would! Campion for constable! Away with Plugg!"

Ben stared at them. It was as if, after Ned's display of rough justice, the Shoreditch folk had suddenly found their voices. No one liked Plugg, but few would have dared tell him so. And now, all eyes were on the man himself.

Slowly, the constable got to his feet. He was a sorry sight. His hat had fallen off, and blood ran down his jerkin. He fumbled in his sleeve and found a dirty kerchief, which he put to his nose. Then, as Ned still stood over him, Plugg turned and surveyed the crowd with a look of disgust.

"You can't dismiss me," he snarled. "I'm appointed by the Justice, to serve for a year. So you're out of luck!"

At that there were more groans – but to Plugg's surprise, Ned merely grinned at him.

"Would that be old Justice Smithers?" he enquired. "Why, he's a customer. I shoe his horse for him, and pull his teeth too. I'll have a word when I see him next – I reckon he'll be interested to hear how you've carried out your duties."

"I'll have a word with him too," Tom Slyte put in. "And I bet any man here an angel that we'll see Ned Campion as constable before the month is out!"

A cheer went up, which drew a muttered curse from James Plugg. But even he could see that the tide had turned against him now. For the last time, he glowered at the crowd.

"Well then – to blazes with the lot of you!" he cried. "Take whoever you like – even a thick-headed blacksmith!"

He was about to go – whereupon a high voice piped up. "My master isn't thick-headed!" Squeaky Martin cried, pushing forward with a half-eaten gingerbread in his hand. "He's twice the man you are – and he can lace his own breeches!"

There was a stunned silence – then everyone shouted with laughter. Ned gave his famous donkey laugh, and cuffed his prentice playfully about the head. Tom Slyte roared and slapped Ned on the back, while Peascod barked furiously. And all James Plugg could do was pick up his hat and stalk off, shoving people aside. Soon he had disappeared, and the crowd closed up again as if he had never been there.

Ben looked round, feeling very cheerful all of a sudden, his own laughter rising. He saw Kate and Meg pushing their way through to see what was going on. Then he turned to Harry Higgs and his prentice, who were standing together. The dragon was back on the puppet master's hand.

Ben smiled at Master Higgs. "I must get back," he said, and nodded to his companion. "Goodbye, Tobias. I wish you luck."

The two young people exchanged looks. Then, without further word, Ben turned to make his way to the stage.

He was still smiling. It had been a turbulent springtime, but all had turned out well in the end, he thought. Now summer stretched ahead, with the prospect of the visit to his family in the country. How the little village of Hornsey would seem to him after his exciting times in London, he wasn't sure. But somehow he knew that more adventures awaited him...if not there, than somewhere else.

Lord Bonner's Men had their instruments tuned, and were waiting for him. As Ben hurried up, John sighed. "I was about to come looking for you," he said. "What were you doing – and what was all the commotion over there?"

Ben climbed onto the stage. "I think they've chosen a new constable," he said, and sat down on his stool. Matt looked at him in surprise.

"And there was a brabble," Ben added, "but no real harm was done."

Then he smiled at his fellow players, and picked up his lute.

About the author

John Pilkington worked in a research laboratory, on a farm, and as a rock guitarist in several bands before realizing he wanted to write. After taking a degree in Drama and English, and acting and directing for a touring theatre company, he began his professional writing career with radio plays. He has since written plays for the theatre and television scripts for the BBC. He is also the author of a series of historical crime novels, and a non-fiction book, *A Survival Guide for Writers*. *Elizabethan Mysteries* is his first series for younger readers.

Born in Lancashire, John now lives in Devon with his partner and son.

Look out for Ben Button's next adventure, coming soon...

Usborne Quicklinks

For links to websites where you can find out more about life in Tudor London, the theatre in Elizabethan times, and the Spanish Armada and the war with Spain, go to the Usborne Quicklinks Website at www.usborne-quicklinks.com and enter the keyword "revenge".

Internet safety

When using the Internet, make sure you follow these safety guidelines:

- Ask an adult's permission before using the Internet.
- Never give out personal information, such as your name, address or telephone number.
- If a website asks you to type in your name or e-mail address, check with an adult first.
- If you receive an e-mail from someone you don't know, don't reply to it.